A Clockwork Flower

Written By Michael Stevens

Spire Mou
Telmara
Armillaria Swamp
Iniko's Hut
Life Tree/ Lost Library
Alden's Ho
Bramblehe
Karnuhim Desert
Forever Fields
Atlant

Wildspitze
Sabalan Mountains
ntains
Tzora Forest
Longmore Forest
Renfrew
Rynfyre Ridge
me
Lake Cath Deiridh
aven
tis

A Clockwork Flower

Book one: Aries Adventure

MICHAEL STEVENS

International Edition: 1

September 2024

Designed and written by Michael Stevens

Hardcover ISBN:979-8-9915649-0-8

Paperback ISBN 979-8-9915649-1-5

Published by M.J. Stevens

Contact Author
P.O. Box 166
Sprague, WA 99032

Michaelmjstevens.com

Dedication

Table of Contents

Prologue

It was early July 27th, an ordinary Tuesday. *Well, at least that's what most people would have seen.* There I was, laying in the Grass in the middle of Manhattan's Central Park.

The effervescence of evaporated water tickling my nose as I stared up at the brightening sky of daybreak. The yellows, oranges and teals filled my eyes with beauty.
To me the world had a certain level of magic. It's just no one paid enough attention.

To them everything is just ordinary, to me the ordinary can easily become the extraordinary with a deep breath and some focus, attention to detail I suppose.
My mom always said, *"Aries get your head out of the clouds, pay attention when I'm talking to you, please."*

I hated this for two reasons, one: She used my real name, since I can remember I made everyone call me Ari. The thing is I hate my name not the name itself but the story behind it.

See my mom teaches history she has her Ph.D. in Mythological studies. When she found out she was pregnant with me, I guess her and my father *(whoever he is)* fought a lot about whether or not to have me. So much so she told him to scram because she was going to have me whether he liked it or not. Well, he did.

Thus, giving her the clever idea of naming me Aries, after the Greek god of war. To her it was the perfect name, to me it's just a reminder I was unwanted before I even had a chance, like a scar on my very soul.

Two: if she only knew how much I actually paid attention. Yeah, I get it I don't hear her when she's talking because I'm so focused on the minor things like the way the coffee smelled. When it's freshly brewed the aroma has a calming effect on my lungs, or the way the sun glinted off the window just right. Making it so you could see the rays of light breakdown into a gradient with the colors of a rainbow.

I guess listening to people talk was at the bottom of my priorities unless I found what they were saying beneficial or stimulating. I assume it's because of my attentive priorities, I was diagnosed with attention deficit disorder when I was a kid.

My mom tried to medicate me. But I refused because the meds made me feel like nothing more than a zombie. She did have something right my head was in the clouds and at this very moment that's exactly where it was.

There was nothing more ethereal than watching an early morning sunrise. The colors of the world are so perfect in that moment. Everything had a glow to it. The stillness of the world quiet and serene. The birds waking with twitters and chirps.

Tick. The breeze rustling the leaves on the trees like a faint chorus of a snare drum.

Tick. The dew of the grass dampening the ground and air simultaneously. *Tick.* The noisy city far from my mind.

Tick. The softness of my heartbeat, with the rise and fall of my breath like a melody.

Tick. "What in the hell is that sound!" I yelled allowed, if any passerby were to see me, they would have thought I was nuts. That ticking was making me nuts. That was for sure it had no place in this moment. I had to find where it was coming from.

I jumped up, racing toward the sound looking high and low, as if I were a panicked rabbit running from the hungry fox. Almost to the bridge I heard the ticking growing louder and louder. It felt as though it was everywhere maybe even inside of me.

My pulse was racing with fear or excitement at this point, I couldn't tell which. Then like a car crash time came to a halt I saw it. A golden glow just under the bridge.

It was an ornate flower, a cross between the inner workings of a clock and a Faberge egg. The flower itself was closed like it hadn't seen the light of day. But beautiful, nonetheless.

I hurriedly plucked it from the ground hiding it with my jacket. I had to study it. I had to see it open. It was the strangest thing. Like I knew this was just the beginning of something bigger than myself.

Chapter 1

FOREVER FIELDS

The run home was a blur of city lights car horns and nameless faces. I didn't have time to take it all in. Only thoughts of this clockwork flower echoed in my head. What is this thing? Who made it? What's inside? And finally, how do I make it bloom.

Reaching the home where my mom and I stayed. It was a nice place it reminded me of a loft and an old firehouse. Windows that let light in, but you couldn't really see out of. I loved it. It was so open with plenty of space.

My mom picked it out just after we moved to Manhattan when I was seven. The brown hardwood floors. The reds and whites of the walls, from the brick and mortar. Some half plastered over. The black wrought iron of the railings.

Man since day one I was in love, like it was my own superhero hideout. So many good memories. I quickly ran to an iron spiral staircase that led to the upstairs. Which resembled an inverted veranda. My room was up there. Or rather my study, because my mind bounced from subject to subject and I'd often hyper fixate on new hobbies.

It was littered with chemistry sets, art supplies, books stacked from floor to ceiling. Along with a wide variety of other tools from my many previously pursued hobbies. I burst through my door.

Tripping over a pile of dirty clothes I clutched my newest prize tight to my chest as I began tumbling toward my writing desk. I landed, not so elegantly into my computer chair. Spinning rapidly before slowing to a stop and sliding out onto my head. I heard something rolling across the hardwood floor and opened my previously wincing eyes.

The Clockwork was teetering to a halt about 3 feet from me. With a groan I collected myself. Rubbing my head as I picked up this curious mechanical flower bulb. I set it on the desk as I dug through the messy top drawer till, I found an old magnifying glass.

Sitting down to take a better look at the clockwork in all its intricacies. I saw right away it was definitely made to open. Each petal had an almost micrometer gap and at their base were latches. I turned it over and overlooking for a button, a switch, a keyhole, anything. Only I was left with more questions than answers, I found nothing.

I fumbled through my chaotically sorted drawer and grabbed for some tweezers. I tried to pull a petal back, but it snapped shut without hesitation. A chisel? Nope wouldn't budge. Aha a soldering iron! Maybe I could take the petals off.

I heated up the pen impatiently, checking it often. "Ouch" I burnt my finger. Carefully I place the tip of the soldering pen to the fine latch, but something strange happened instead of the latch melting, the tip began to melt away backwards till it disappeared altogether. Almost as if the flower super-heated the soldering iron itself.

I spent hours trying to get this clockwork to do my bidding. I tried a micro screwdriver, no screws. Chemical reaction, no damage to the flower but it did leave a sizable hole in my writing desk.

My best attempt was tacking wire loops to the table, in order to pull several petals down. I managed to get four out of what looked like fifty pulled back, and the damn clockwork flower snapped shut with such force it jumped off the writing desk sealing itself shut again. I got so frustrated at this point. I took a hammer with a running start and tried to smash the flower and that's when things got even weirder. As soon as the hammer made contact or would have made contact it was propelled through the air by a blindingly bright blue light.

As it went flying through the air, the hammer hit my bedroom door. Implanting itself into its thick wooden face. Trying to retrieve my hammer was like trying to pull Excalibur from the stone. I could literally pull myself up with it. Finally, by planting both my feet onto the door and pulling with my whole body I retrieved my hammer and fell backwards onto the floor.

Laying there I gazed upward to the ceiling of my room. That's when I saw it. Letters made of blue light hovering just inches from my ceiling. They looked like they were written in futhark or something similar.

I scrambled to my feet. I knew I had a book on Norse and Gaelic. I quickly copied the letters down before I began my search. Looking through piles of books with every variation of runic language I could think of, nothing matched.

Frustrated and feeling defeated, I banged my head against the top of my writing desk. The vibrating rattled the wall, and the hanging bookcase just above me. Filled with childhood books. The rattle sent a half-hazard laying book tumbling down with a **Crack** onto the desk. Laying open cover side up. I read the Title. *Faeries, Fae, and Magical Beings.* I picked it up.

I remember I was fond of the pictures though; I don't think I ever actually read the thing, but it's what got me into art to begin with. Seeing all the elves, gnomes, fairies, and pixies illustrated so well. They were almost lifelike. However, when I turned it over there was a grid with runes the title of which read, *The magical alphabet of the fae translation guide.*

THIS WAS IT! I spent the next hour getting the translation.

" Human destruction doesn't blossom or create. Only the sweetness of the fae can open the gate."

Whatever that meant, but it's a start. I began thumbing through the book. Fae sweetness? What is that? It's got to be in here. Nisse and Tomte like porridge and butter, brownies prefer bread and butter, pixies like pears and mallow fruit, faeries like saffron, sweet butter, milk, honey, sweetcakes. Hmm it's a long shot but I'll try it.

I ran and grabbed the honey that we left in the center of the white granite countertop of the kitchen island. *"Well, this is possibly the dumbest idea I've had all night"* I spoke allowed to myself looking at the clock, 2 Am *"oh that would be why."* I smirked with decision. As I let a drop of honey fall in slow motion to the center of the clockwork.

Nothing; well back to the book, I grabbed it and turned around. A bright blue light filled the room again only this time it sucked me backwards. As the portal swallowed me in. I can only imagine that Clockwork Flower snapping shut again. As I came to a screeching halt in a field of purple grass. I heard a snickering behind me.

"*Ooohooo, aha hello ha-ha and welcome to the forever fields ha-ha-ha.*" A blue imp resembling one of the creatures I saw in the book earlier. He was sitting on a signpost in the middle of the field. Though there were no roads. So why a signpost? "*If you're wondering why, it's called the forever fields aha. It's because you've been sitting on your butt forever ha-ha. The names Grip. What's yours smelly*"?

I scrambled to my feet. Brushing the strange grass off of my pants. I looked around bewildered and amazed. My new surroundings were like nothing I had ever seen before. Purple rolling grass fields, orange skies and mushrooms as tall as the trees. The trees themselves bore what looked like every fruit imaginable, instead of one or the other. The air was filled with weird and new sounds. Along with scents I couldn't recognize but delighted in. Everything here was so different and so refreshing.

"*Achem, well boy?*" The impatient imp Grip had said, picking his very long blue nose. His bulbous head tilted backward, his red colored clean cut mohawk was the same color as the sign he sat upon. Letting his mouth hang open. His even longer tongue lulling from side to side, obviously enjoying the excavation of his nose a little too much. He hocked a bright green glob onto a nearby white almost translucent bush.

I snapped back to the present situation and spoke boldly as if not to seem afraid. "*Aries D'Angelo Lacroix, at your service*" "*Ha-ha, Stupid Surfacer, don't you know anything. Never give your name to the Fae.*" A wide and malevolent grin stretched from one pointed and pierced ear to the other.

He pointed at me with his long knobby fingers, his fingernails a yellow brown having a similar look of woodgrain and sharp. With his other hand he grabbed a potion bottle filled with a purple liquid from his belt. Tossing it toward me. Hitting the ground, the bottle broke causing a chemical reaction as the liquid turned to a gas it rose up and engulfed me in its purple vapors.

It was then I felt a click on my wrists. When the gaseous cloud had cleared, I saw my wrists were bound in a medieval like form of handcuffs. Only they weren't a typical iron they were made of a strange steel I was unfamiliar with. Linked together by a chain, with a lead from me to my captor.

"No, you can't! I Didn't know! I don't even know where I am!" I pleaded with Grip. *"Stop shouting Surfacer, your mine now. You will do as I say!"* He barked back. *"Please, at least tell me where I am."* I begged, allowing my fear to show. *"Fine then, if you must know. You're in Underhill."* Grip responded in a matter-of-fact way. *"Underhill"*? I questioned, still uncertain of where or even when I was.

"Yes, yes. You surfacers have given us many names over the years, The center of the earth, The Underworld, Lumeria, Tir Na Nog, Mag Mel, Fairyland, Elfhiem, and possibly the most stupid name of all Wonderland". Grip spoke increasingly agitated. Spitting again at the word wonderland.

"Those can't all be the same place, can they?" I asked more confused than before. *"Yes, they can, and they are. See, you stupid surfacers come down here through caves, tunnels, and sinkholes and each of you think you're the first one to lay eyes on the place and decide to make up some stupid name.*

Instead of just asking. But that's a surfacer for ya, always trying to control things. That's why we left the surface in the first place." Grip began to rant he must have had a lot pent up.

I couldn't believe it, a whole world just under our noses. This whole time. It held such beauty and was magnificent. Except for my captor of course, he on the other hand was quite an odd fellow. The more he talked however the less frightened I got.

"-and that silly little girl went around eating the mushrooms and hallucinating because she found out she can't eat the food here or she would get stuck, she had no rhyme or reason, and can you believe she kept mistaking me for a cat? The nerve. And all this business about a red queen trying to take her head, how stupid she'd feel if she realized she was just standing there frighted of a tavern sign for hours on end muttering to herself. Had to make her chase a rabbit back to the surface. Dumb girl."

He couldn't be serious. Well at least he wasn't paying any attention to me, maybe I could escape. I began to back up. The handcuffs sent a shockwave through me, and I cried out. *"Not going to work boy, magic binding. Silly No nothing surfacer."* Grip said nonchalantly as he hopped down from the signpost and came hobbling toward me. *"STOP CALLING ME THAT! YOU CAN CALL ME ARI! I AM NOT STUPID EITHER!"* I bellowed with a mix of pain and frustration. *"Hmmmm, that remains to be seen.... Ari"* My captor spoke with a laugh.

"Come now, it's time we were off, I can fetch a pretty price for a surfacer slave with the blacksmith in Bramblehaven."

He said pulling the chain lead. Though he was only as tall as my knee he was as strong as a full-grown man. The pull was more than I expected, and it jerked me forward into a stumble.

"Now tell me Ari, how did you fall from the sky? When most surfacers come through caves, I haven't seen that before." Grip questioned looking over his shoulder as we got onto a dirt path. Following the signs arrow to Bramblehaven. *"Well, I'm not exactly sure. There was this Clockwork Flower and I..."* *"Clockwork flower you say"?* The imp interrupted looking nervous. Beads of green sweat appeared on his forehead as he began looking around for something.

  "That's enough of your lies surfacer!" He burst out and pulled hard on the chain forcing me to stumble again. *"It's not a lie!"* I protested. *"No more out of you till we reach Bramblehaven!"* His demeanor changed completely. I squinted my eyes. Knowing there's something more behind his sudden behavior and I'm going to find out exactly what it is.

Clockwork Flower

The Forever Fields-

Ari's entry point into Underhill. The mysterious and fantastical subterranean world.

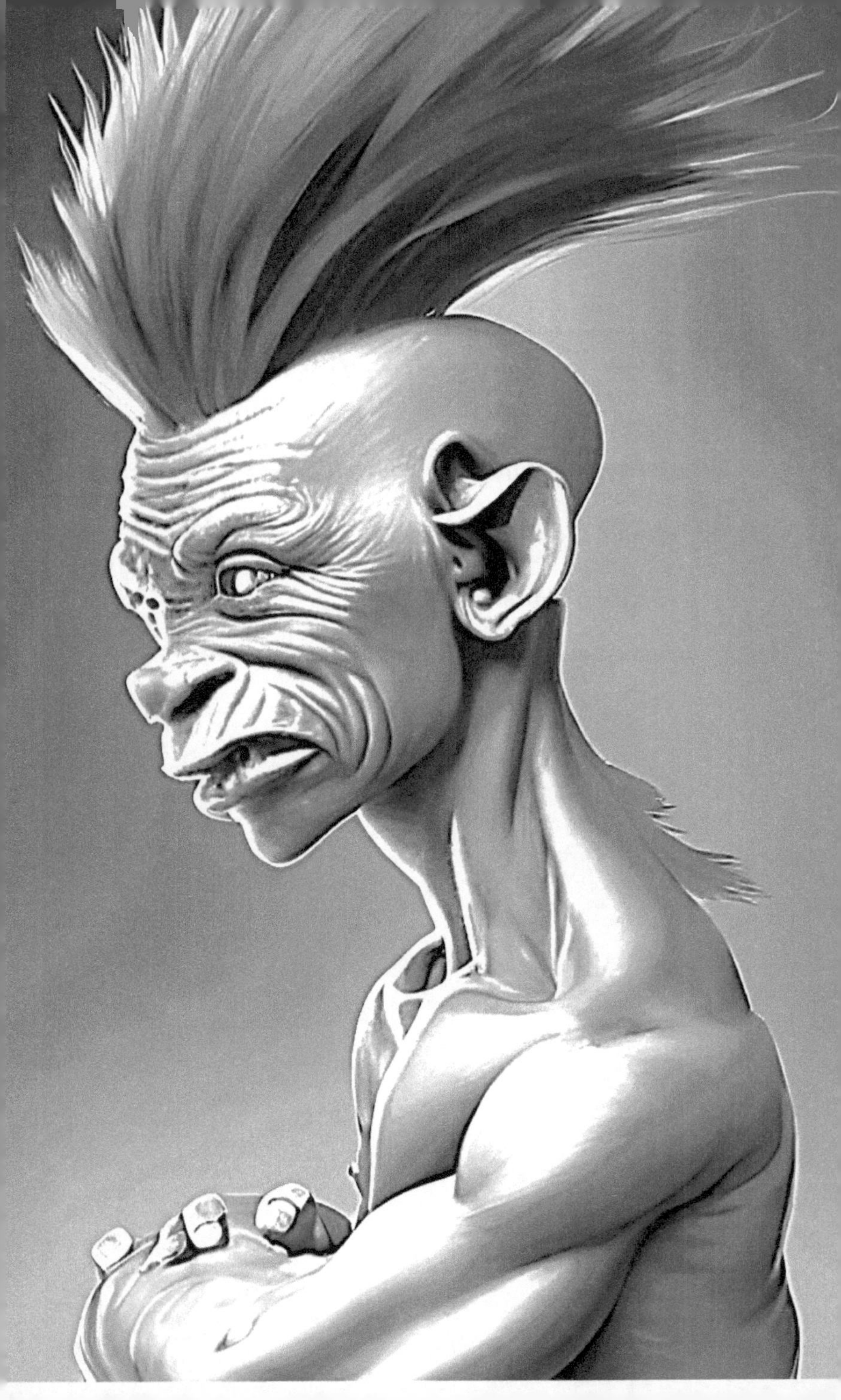

Grip- *The Imp*

Chapter 2

BRAMBLEHAVEN

Grip pulled me by my chain bindings into the small fey village of Bramblehaven. A village with a quaint capacity. Stone huts with gnarled root like, thatch roofing. Cabins made of thick lumber. Teepees that were made from huge bones and tied with thick black hair.

A combination of what seemed like many cultures, a melting pot of the fey kind. A mix of childhood daydream and nightmare. Imagination personified into a town unlike any I had ever seen.

There were merchant stalls selling their wares, totems, scrolls, potion bottles, shrunken heads, sweet smelling breads and berries. The population looked to be made up of goblins, fairies, sprites, dryads, nymphs, sylphs, dwarves, hags, and countless other beings. That I had never seen with my own eyes, other than in childhood books.

We came to a stop in front of an open-faced hut. A glow of hot ember and molten lava emanating from the rear. The sound of metal clanks and bangs rattled my ears.

Grip gave a hard tug on the chain. It forced me to sprawl into the dusty and cracked clay road. A cloud of dust filled my mouth as I gasped from the hard blow. Hitting the ground, I looked up at my captor. A malevolent grin on his face.

"Sit, stay, good surfacer!" He latched my chain to a post outside. How degrading to be treated like nothing more than a dog. I watched as Grip entered the building. He puffed his chest out and began to saunter to the back.

A huge figure emerged from the shadows. Wearing what looked like leather overalls carrying ingots of metal in every shade of the rainbow. His long brown hair and braided beard framed his very round face; only his bulbous nose, rounded cheeks and bright fluorescent blue eyes shone through, the copious amount of hair this oversized man had. I assumed this was the Dwarf Grip had mentioned.

I could see them talking. The Dwarf dropped the ingots to the ground clapping dust from his hands as he bellowed a huge laugh. Grip looked around nervously his face turned to a lavender. I could almost swear he had the look of embarrassment about him. The two walked toward me. Grip strayed behind looking at his feet and rubbing the back of his Mohawk like he was ashamed. The face of the Dwarf stooped down to see me, and he smiled. Laughing he grabbed me by the back of the shirt and lifted me to my feet.

"Ello, Little one, a bit lost, are we? Seems you've been tricked by our friend here. Lucky for you he brought ya to one of the few honest blacksmiths in all of Underhill." A look of confusion passed over my face. *"Tricked?"* I asked with hesitation. *"Aye tricked lad"* he winked as he said this.

"Thelgrim Hammerstone pleasure to meet yer acquaintance, see though Ol' Grip has a point. Ya shouldn't tell a fey yer name. He ain't exactly fey kind. More goblin kind really their close cousins' goblins n' imps ya see. So, he don't own ya like a fey would nothing more than a smoke bomb and a slide a hand. Imps are tricky devils." My eyes burned with anger as I stared Grip down over Thelgrim's shoulder. He covered his head and dove behind the counter of Thelgrim's shop.

"Now, Grip informed me he lost the key, when he offered to sell ya to me. And seeing how yer not his to sell, and I don't need help in me shop, how about we set ya free." He pulled

a pointed hammer from his tool belt; He had barely tapped the metal binding with a small flick of his wrist. Causing the metal to burst like it was made of nothing more than fine China. *"Ha, Goblin steal. May as well be worthless"* Thelgrim said heartily.

    "I HEARD THAT!" A green boil covered goblin staring from an adjacent blacksmith stall spat. *"Nothing that ain't true Bloodbog, that right boyo?"* He patted my back. The kind gesture felt like a sledgehammer. I choked on the air escaping my lungs. Not wanting to be in this awkward exchange, and unsure of what to say I made a face somewhere in between a grimace of pain and a smirk.

    The goblin Bloodbog just stared hollow eyed. Working his jaw like a cow chewing cud before spitting a tar like goop to the clay ground. I couldn't seem to look away. Bloodbog scooped up the clay and Black tar mixture with a garden spade. Slopping it into a mold, on a bed of coal. He shook his head.

    Getting my bearings back I remembered that stupid frustrating imp who had been degrading me for hours on the way to this village. My face grew hot with anger as I bolted for him, revenge on my mind. Suddenly I was running in midair as I realized, Thelgrim had picked me up by the back of the shirt again and had me dangling over the ground.

    "Feisty bugger aren't ya, anyway slow down little one. Forgive him it's his nature. Trickster at heart." Thelgrim said in his kind but booming voice. *"Let me down!"* I quipped in frustration. *"Not till ya promise ta not hurt our friend there."* the Dwarf smiled *"He's no friend of mine!"* I shouted and tried running in place again. *"That may be so, but he could be, things are often not what they seem down here, so promise."* Thelgrim

wisely spoke. *"Fine, I promise just put me down!"* I gave in knowing I'd be stuck in the air if I hadn't.

Grip's head popped up from behind the counter shaking like a cold chihuahua. He put his hands up like he was under arrest. *"See not so bad he's just a frightened fella, now he said ya came to us in a peculiar way. Come inside an have a chat. Let's see what we can make of your story."* Thelgrim said pointing at Grip and ushering me inside.

Walking into the blacksmiths shop was an otherworldly feeling, I mean obviously it was, but the awe I was feeling was indescribable. Any other explanation falls short.

We made our way to the back of the shop where there was a square table with intricate Celtic like designs carved from leg to tabletop, seemingly filled with gold. It paired well with the deep red of the wood that the table was made from. We sat across from one another.

Grip scrambled in like a surprised and frightened cat. Knocking things over as he dashed through the room with two mugs setting them on the table. *"So, Grip tells me you traveled here by clockwork, is this true?"* Thelgrim asked with a pointed stare. *"Well yeah, I found this flower under the bridge..."* *"The flower, hmmm interesting."* Thelgrim interrupted me mid-sentence. *"Did it call to you, boy?"* Thelgrim asked in a hushed tone like it was a life-or-death situation. *"What do you mean, call to me?"* I inquired, getting the feeling the Dwarf knew more about the curious flower than I did. *"I MEAN DID YOU HEAR IT BEFORE YOU SAW IT?"* He boomed, before looking around like he made some mistake. *"Well, did you?"* He followed up with a whisper. *"Y-y-yeah"* I stammered, starting to feel anxious about this whole thing.

What did I get myself into? To my amazement Thelgrim grinned like a child on Christmas day. *"Your hands boy, let me see your hands."* I hesitantly put my hands out. This was the first time I even looked at a part of me since I got here. As I turned my palms over, I saw a glowing green circular light right in the center of my palm. *"Ahhh!"* I shrieked, pulling my hand back and shaking it vigorously. Trying to put out the nonexistent flame or bee-sting. However, my hand kept on glowing. The circular light had some sort of design inside. Quite like a seal of Solomon I had seen in one of my metaphysical books I kept at home.

Thelgrim grabbed my hand quickly. Hushing me, looking over his shoulder, almost as if he felt eyes upon him. *"Yes, this is it."* He said to himself as he pressed his giant thumb into my palm. It turned the glowing green light into golden streams that burst from my hand. I watched as the golden light lit Thelgrim's face. I looked on with a mix of horror and awe. The flower materialized in my hand slowly at first, like golden Tetris cubes falling into place. Until it became the entirety of the mysterious clockwork flower that sent me here. Almost as soon as it fully appeared, floating mere inches from my palm. The glowing stopped and it fell bobbling into my hand. In a simultaneous instant, as if someone had just flipped off a light switch.

Thelgrim reached down and picked up the curious object between his forefinger and thumb. It was small in comparison to the dwarves' massive, calloused hands. He smiled again, shaking his head before placing it back into my hand. *"They did it, I can't believe they actually did it."* He said to himself quietly without taking his eyes from the Clockwork. *"Who did what?"* I was puzzled at all this new fragmented information. Letting out a heavy sigh he took a drink from his mug, casting his eyes to the right. He stared into the glow of the fireplace. *"To understand that you'll have to get an Underhill history lesson."* He began.

"Long ago, we lived on the surface world, but the surfacers hunted many of us. Thinking we are beasts or trying to steal our magic away. Surfacers have always been afraid of what they don't understand, and they think they can gain that understanding by control, so they'd capture some of us and put us to work. In whatever they felt best paired with our magical ability. Till the kings of old decided our kind would be safer elsewhere. So, they carved out a new home beneath the soil and rock. But even though we separated ourselves from the surface. We found ourselves advancing when your civilizations advanced. We walked parallel to your world. Until you sought to destroy yourselves with your wars and your bombs. Then some of us decided to go back to the old ways like here in Bramblehaven." He paused to take another drink and he looked at me with sadness in his eyes.

"But some of our kin became obsessed with advancements. Far from here in the city of Telmara. Where magic and technology become symbiotic. A very different kind of dwarves live. They call themselves the Dwartin. They're good-natured folk just have an affinity for this new symbiosis. They created 7 clockworks. The Flower" He nodded toward me *"The*

sword, The shield, The locket, the key, the bangle and the bowl. It is said that they gave each of these to the faeries who frequently travel between your world and ours through their fairy rings. They were to scatter them across the globe, and one day these talismans would call the guardians to save our world and theirs."

In disbelief I blurted out questioning Thelgrim. *"Guardians? Save the world?" "Yeah, kiddo."* An unfamiliar voice. Came from the stairway behind Thelgrim. I looked up. As I heard a strange sound following the disembodied voice.

> *"Teepees that were made from huge bones and tied with thick black hair."*

*Bramblehaven-*Town view

*Bramblehaven-*Market St.

Thelgrim - Dwarven Blacksmith

Chapter 3

ALUWYN

The sound reminded me of the dragonflies of summer, stealing the dewdrops from the leaves. In the early morning sunrise. The sound belonged to a pixie, who was now making her way down the stairs. Buzzing and about the same size as the dragonflies I remembered fondly. She flew right up to my face before pinching my nose with both of her tiny hands. I reached up and grabbed at my nose. *"Ow, what the hell was that for?"* I exclaimed, and at the same time I had this knee jerk reaction.

The tiny pixie evaporated in a cloud of smoke before reappearing in front of me at a normal human sized height, leaning onto the table. She giggled *"Just saying hi, what's the big deal?"* She looked like she had just gotten back from an 80's punk rock concert. Torn acid washed jeans and a cutoff Ramones t-shirt. She had spiked bracelets to match her equally spiky black hair. "Next time say hi without trying to rip my nose off ok." I spoke with irritation.

She smirked, rolling her eyes. Straightening her posture before turning, giving me a wave to brush away my comment. *"Oh, stop whining ya big baby, what kinda guardian can't handle a pinch on the nose? Honestly, it's embarrassing."* I pushed my chair back and stood up *"I'm not a guardian."* My voice wavered. I was uncertain of anything at this point. She turned around to face me, her dragonfly-like wings fluttering quickly, making her spin around even faster as she flew back toward my direction. *"That's not what that little trinket in your hand says, it says you're a guardian, so get used to it!"* *"Fine, but I don't know what that means. What's your problem anyway? And why are you dressed like that?"* I shot back.

Her face morphed with anger, her skin turned from a pale white to a deep red and her green eyes went as black as night. *"WHAT'S WRONG WITH THE WAY I DRESS!"* Her shout echoed. *"N-n-nothing, it's just everyone else I've seen down here haven't been dressed as modern."* I stammered. Her demeanor returned to normal at the blink of an eye. *"Thanks, toots I pride myself on keeping up to date. Besides I've been to the surface more times than, well, pretty much anyone. I can't seem to stay away."* she said with elation.

"Being a guardian, means you're gonna save us from the big baddie, duh!" she rolled her eyes again. For someone who could be so small she sure had a big attitude. *"And who is that exactly?"* I raised my eyebrow. *"Hitler"* she said nonchalantly. *"Hitler, like World War 2 Hitler? That Hitler but he's dead"* I said truly in disbelief now. *"Nope wrong again sugar, he's immortal and he lives here in Underhill. And you and the others are gonna stop him from enslaving us and destroying the planet."* *"What!? Are you crazy? How?"* I said flailing my arms like an awkward chicken.

"I wouldn't call her that if I were you." Grip interrupted *"m-m-my mistake."* I stuttered. *"You get a pass this time toots, and it's a long story, let's talk and walk. C'mon I know the perfect place."* She said turning and beckoning me to follow.

We walked for a while, through the quaint fey village. Till we reached the outskirts where there was a small river blooming with greenery. Small birds chirped alongside strange sounds I'd never heard before. We had stopped here. A giant ladybug-like insect came sauntering down from the nearby stalagmite mountains, I watched it pass in awe. I'd never seen a bug the size of a Buick. Much less one that was a cross between a ladybug and a great horned beetle.

"Awe shucks, I better tell Helena her Ladyvine got out again." The pixie said with a crinkle on her nose. *"But that can wait. You see above that spire."* She pointed far into the distance. I followed her gesture with my gaze to a large spire. Above it was a purple vortex, its crackling of electrically charged ions barely audible from where we stood.

It looked terrifying. The purple wisps and cloud formations reminded me of some far-off galaxy; only in the center instead of some bright star was a black hole. *"That's how he got here, it's right above the biggest city in Underhill, Telmara."* The pixie said sadness welling in her eyes. *"But why here, why Underhill and how did he make that!?"* I shouted pointing at the vortex. *"I don't know, all I can say is all his investigation into the paranormal led him here, and now he is enslaving our kind!"* She shouted back, this was when I realized the light seemed to fade. Like the dark clouds of the vortex were somehow reaching us. The winds were picking up.

I looked to my new friend and saw terror in her eyes now. I glanced behind me following her gaze and understood. Above us wasn't some torrential storm, but a giant dragon staring right at us, the wind coming from every beat of its gigantic wings. Teeth dripping with slime, falling to the ground beneath it. I could barely make-out the titanium band around its enormous neck. A small square blue light blinking on the left side is what gave it away. *"Run!"* She screamed already in motion.

I followed but fumbled and fell. I heard the flames scorch the earth behind me. I felt the heat nip at the soles of my shoes. I scrambled to my feet catching up to my counterpart. She slid on the ground like a major league baseball player sliding into home. She grabbed a concealed latch on the desert like ground and pulled open a trap door we jumped in closing it behind us. A furious roar followed our descent into the crawl space. She pressed a finger to my lips hushing my racing mind from pouring out from between them. We sat in silence and listened to its thunderous and confused roars till finally, the last wing beat died off into the distance.

" Was that a freaking dragon, dragons are real too!?" *"Where have you been under a rock, yes, everything the human mind has written about or imagined is real in some form or another."* She said in a snooty tone *"Look we almost died try to be a little nicer, I mean I don't even know your name."* I said still in frantic disbelief.

"It's Aluwyn." she said looking back as she opened the hatch and flew out of the dugout. I climbed the rickety rope ladder and followed Aluwyn out. What little plant life there was, was gone. The earth was black. The passing Ladyvine from earlier was nothing but a hollow shell floating in a melted puddle of its own insides. Beside the pool, Aluwyn sat crying. I walked up to her slowly placing my hand onto her soot covered shoulder. She wiped her tears trying to hide her pain. *"Let's get this mess cleaned up."* She walked to the river and began to move her hands like she was conducting a concerto.

The water began to float into the air as she guided them to the surrounding fires. I helped with a wooden bucket I found beside the river. It was nearly night when the last ember died out. I was distracted staring at the clockwork flower, I'd pulled it from my pocket wondering how I'm meant to save them. Trying to wipe of the soot and blackness from its intricacies.

"We should wash up to." Aluwyn's voice echoed as it brought me back to the present moment. *"Your probably right."* I said feeling exhausted. I placed the clockwork back into my pocket. She grabbed my hand and we waded into the river.

When we got in waist deep something unimaginable happened. Green and gold light began to surround me. Glowing beneath the water. Aluwyn stepped back. The light was coming from my pocket.

I pulled the clockwork out again. Its petals began unfolding as more light came pouring out. I dropped it stunned, and it began to float like a little golden lotus. Swirling beams of light danced in every direction. It cascaded over the burnt plants and scorched ground.

It reminded me of the northern lights I had seen on a documentary about Alaska once. To our amazement, the plants and earth began to come back to life slowly at first. And then remarkably even the once dry ground began to fill with grass and flowers. It not only healed it from the dragon's damage but fertilized it with new life.

A sound came from our right like a cross between a moo and a purr, as a six footed, solo stampede headed in our direction. Aluwyn's face alight with delight. As she flew to meet up with the revived Ladyvine. Looking around me in every direction I said the only thing that came to mind. *"Woah...*

Aluwyn- Pixie

City of Telmara-

Biggest city in Underhill, The epicenter of evil

...

Underhill Dragon

Chapter 4

LOCKET AND KEY

I was still pretty shaken up from our encounter with that fire-breathing monstrosity. My hands trembled as I lifted a glass of Centurion Cider. The barkeep told me his kind invented it, by stomping their four hooves over fermented fruit. While he dusted the shelves behind him with his horse-like tail. *"I didn't know centaurs wore glasses."* I said feeling a bit fuzzy inside at this point, one too many ciders I suppose.

Obviously, the barkeep took offense. His long hair snapped the air like a whip. As he turned his head quickly in my direction. He leaned forward till he was eyelevel with me. Looking just over the brim of his rounded spectacles. *"I didn't know all surfacers where so daft."* He chortled, adding in a, *"oh wait yes I did!"* with a snort of air that ruffle my hair. *"Your eyesight might not be any good, but your lungs work great."* I mumbled. He shot me a glare but let me be.

I spun on the bar stool and went over to Aluwyn, Thelgrim, and Grip who were throwing axes at a target. Laughing amongst one another like old friends. Then again, I guess they were. Thelgrim and Grip anyway.

Aluwyn was Thelgrim's adopted daughter. He told me he found her in and old silver mine. At first, I guess he had thought she was a gem. So small and bright but, when he picked her up, he could just make out her tiny features.

"It wasn't long till she learned how to change size and, that's when she learned to get into trouble!" He spoke of it with a laugh that brought a tear to his eye. I could tell they all shared some fond memories. Which is why I felt like even more of an outsider. Walking up to them in the middle of their game.

"Hey Ari, wanna play?" Grip spoke moving around like an orangutan. He had loosened up a lot since we had first met. Just days ago. *"Sure"* I said, grabbing a throwing axe. I lifted it in a mock manner from watching them. I had never actually done any kind of sport. I aimed at the target; my body swayed from side to side.

Come to think of it, I had never drank before. Back home I wasn't old enough, but down here the laws were different. I tried to steady myself as I pulled my arm back to throw. A loud bang erupted as the front door flew open startling me. I let go of the ax. It flew wildly around the room banging off shields that adorned the walls. It spun rapidly around a chandelier made of antlers before releasing itself.

It whirled straight for the bespectacled barkeep. The centaur ducked. As the axe split open a very expensive looking bottle on the back wall. The barkeep reared up slamming his front hooves onto the counter, making himself look even more immense. *"You're cut off!"* He shouted in a shrill tone.

I looked to my right to see who was coming inside. It was two hooded figures with daggers on their left thighs. One was cloaked in a deep purple and the other in a royal blue. They were slender and agile looking, about my height as well. All the commotion from my desperate attempt to fit in made me stick out even more like a sore thumb. The purple cloaked figure followed the centaurs pointing hand and mad gaze straight to me. Under the purple hood, I saw glowing honey brown eyes and flowing cinnamon colored hair. In that short glance, I noticed her hair perfectly framed a small silver heart shaped locket made from gears.

Time sped up again. I tugged at Thelgrim's sleeve. *"I think she has another clockwork!"* I pointed at the shrouded woman who was making her way to her companion. The blue cloaked figure lifted a bag from his belt and motioned to the barkeep to approach. I could see he had jewelry on as well. A golden bracelet with a small key hanging from it, only the teeth of the key kept morphing and changing. It had to be a clockwork.

I couldn't believe it. I looked to Thelgrim; He must have seen it too because his Dwarven mouth was hanging open in disbelief. He began to march straight for them. The woman saw him and must have seen this gentle giant as a threat, because she tapped her partner on the shoulder. Who glanced quickly in our direction before grabbing the bag from the counter. They began a frantic and mad dash down the hallway toward the back door of the tavern.

Thelgrim kept after them, Aluwyn, Grip and I close behind. The chase was on. *"Wait, we just wanna talk!"* Thelgrim shouted, but it was of no use, they kept running. We followed them outside. They had somehow seemingly disappeared into thin air.

The alley was empty, quiet, and dark. Some dirt fell onto my head. I brushed it off before looking up. I saw a boot pulling itself onto the roof carefully before disappearing altogether. Aluwyn gave me a silent nod and flew up after them.

As Aluwyn flew up over the roof I could hear her yell *"Stop!"* Thelgrim grabbed Grip and I by the back of our belts. With his mighty hands he swung us into the air. Grip landed gracefully onto the roof, drawing a dagger in each hand simultaneously. *"Or we'll slice you to ribbons!"* He snarled attempting to finish Aluwyn's sentence. I on the other hand fell face first and skidded to a stop. Aluwyn looked back at us. *"Grip, it's not that kind of chase. Put the daggers away."* She spoke in a Stern tone looking back at the two cloaked figures.

Aluwyn hushed her voice. *"We just want to talk; I have a feeling we're on the same side."* The hooded figures looked at us. The smaller of the two giggled at the sight of me laying in a heap. They turned to one another and nodded. The tallest one lifted his bracelet and removed the Clockwork key. The mysterious pair moved their clockworks in unison toward one another. The key began to morph and change to fit the hole on the intricate clockwork locket. When they combined them. They spoke simultaneously.

"With lock and key, when turned to three, will unlock the secrets you keep."

Then with three clicks. Purple smoke jettisoned from within the tiny locket. It encircled the roof. They turned silently toward us standing ominously like statues. The small purple cloaked figure pointed at me still laying on the roof. *"You outsider, speak your truth."* she spoke. Before I could stop myself, the words poured out of my mouth with a groan. *"I think I pissed myself."* Grip started to laugh aloud while everyone else at least tried to stifle theirs.

"You, imp state your intentions!" The tall man in a blue cloak spoke in seriousness. *"I'm not very good at reading social cues, I try to help but I make big messes. I want to be good, but people see my skin before my heart."* He blurted out; followed by *"Blech, how dare you make me say that!"* Grip turned purple

with embarrassment. This time I laughed. *"And you, pixie, your truth?"* The man spoke brushing off our silly display. *"We need your help, we are trying to save Underhill toots, you two and him-"* pointing to me *"-carry three of the seven clockworks said to be the key to our freedom! Will you help us or not, sug?"*

"We will help, but it isn't safe here. He has eyes everywhere." The man said, kneeling. *"We have a safe house hidden a few miles west of town. Take the west road till you come to a life tree. Tap the tree 3 times, it'll show you the way."* The two then took a running start and jumped from the building. Reappearing on a black Pegasus they began flying west and out of sight.

"That's that." Grip said, clapping his hands together like he was trying to get dirt off them. He went over and unrolled a rope ladder. Once on the ground we filled Thelgrim in. We decided it would be best to gather supplies and make the trip at dawn.

Back at Thelgrim's shop, I went upstairs to change. Thelgrim thought some of his childhood clothing may fit me. I found a red and gold tunic and some pants. Fastening them, they were a little baggy but would do.

Descending the stairs, I could see that they were all packed up. Multiple bags covered the large oaken table. *"Let's get some rest, we will head out at first light. We'll need to swing by the stalls and get a ride. Then we will get acquainted with our new friends. Off to bed with yeh."* With that, Thelgrim doused the fire.

I laid on a cot upstairs but found I couldn't sleep. My mind raced with questions. Wondering if any of this was real. Just a few weeks ago I had a normal life in Manhattan.

I wondered how mom was doing, and if she was searching for me. I hoped she was doing ok. I wondered if I could really do this. I didn't really feel like a hero. Before I knew it, my thoughts became so loud it was overwhelming. I had to get up. A walk might help settle my mind.

Getting dressed once again I headed downstairs. The air was crisp with a lightness to it. Surprisingly the night didn't get very dark in Underhill, due to its phosphorescent glow from the rocks and minerals that scattered the ground. I walked up to the river where Aluwyn and I encountered that nightmare of a dragon. I shuddered, recalling it.

The still air began to ring like a thousand wind chimes jingling simultaneously. Barely audible, my attention focused on where it was coming from. I saw something in the distance. A blue ball of light dancing up and down, and bobbing left to right. I'd read about these. They were called wisps and were rare. It's said if you follow them, they will guide you to where you need to be. So, naturally I began to follow it down the road.

It took a sharp turn into a forest of strange trees. I peered under a branch before ducking inside, and into the strange forest. I followed the wisp for some time, but when we came into a clearing it just vanished. Popping much like a bubble made of soap and water would.

In the clearing was a small grassy knoll. Light shone through the trees bathing the hill with an ethereal glow. The light began flickering and then vanished just for a moment. Above me

came a loud screech. My heart began to pound as something big
descended downward, toward the hill and, toward me.

Tavern Bartender

Clockwork Locket

Clockwork Key

Ari and the Wisp

Chapter 5

ALDEN

I was terrified. Did the dragon come back to finish me off? I didn't know if it was too late to hide. I quickly concealed myself behind a boulder, that was jutting out from the grassy knoll. I watched stupefied as the beast descended.

When it landed, it made no sound, light and graceful. The light of the moon shone through the trees. I could see the beast in its full glory. Though I had no idea what it was. It had the head of a bird; its stag-like antlers were prominent and large. Glinting with the sharpness of a well-honed steel dagger. Its forefront remained stag-like from its chest to its cloven hooved forefeet. However, it's back end was like an eagle's, large taloned back legs and a plumed tail. Its lengthy wings rested flush against its side, as it stood atop the knoll. The beasts fur looked like moss, with its brown and green coloration. Its feathers blended well with its soft but spiky fur. The creatures plumage, ranged from brown to an opalescent white. It was unlike anything I'd ever seen.

"Come out boy, I can smell your fear. Not only that but your footing isn't stable, you're going to slip." A voice echoed in my head. As the voice spoke to me, I lost my balance falling backward. Not sure if this beast was a friend or foe, I grabbed a loose rock before shooting upright. *"Drop the stone. I maybe a peryton in appearance but I won't be dining on your heart boy, my father raised me better than that."* The peryton spoke telepathically to me.

Peryton? Eat my heart? Father? I was aghast with confusion. *"Ah a simpleton, come closer boy. I am Alden, lord of this forest. My race is known to be twisted and depraved. However, I am only a half-breed. My father was from the noble race of the gryphons. He raised me like a gryphon, taught me right from wrong, and gave me the ability to speak."* Alden transferred his thoughts to me. *"And how do I know you won't eat my heart like you said?"* I spoke nervously, taking a small step forward. *"Because boy if I were going to eat your heart, I would have done so already. We perytons are remarkably quick. If it were my brother Aliester you would not be so lucky. Check my shadow if you like."* Alden spoke, turning his body to the side as his shadow cast onto the ground.

Its shape was very different from his own appearance. It looked rather like a bunny. *"I. I... I don't understand, it's a rabbit."* I said darting my eyes between Alden and his shadow. I looked to my hand it was still raised clutching the stone, after careful consideration I let it fall to the ground.

"My kind's shadow depicts our last meal. Normally that would be a human. It's somewhat of a delicacy I'm told. I however eat rabbit. Which may be why I haven't gone mad like most perytons. You humans and your chemical and junk filled blood. I believe that is why my kind eventually falls to insanity. But enough of that. Why have you come to my domain? Did the villagers send yet another to try and kill me, as they so often do?"

It appears Alden had his own worries. *"No!"* I said frantically. *"You see I couldn't sleep and there was a wisp. I followed it here and then it disappeared. That's when you came."* I said looking back at Alden's rabbit like shadow. Which seemed to take on a life of its own. Gliding on the knoll as if it were hopping around.

"I see." His voice boomed in my head. *"We are fated then. I will honor this as my father would, tell me boy what is your endeavor? What do you seek? Where is your path taking you?"* Alden pried. *"I guess I'm a guardian, I'm supposed to save all of Underhill. But I really don't see how."* I droned as I scratched the back of my head. Disbelieving my own understanding. *"Well then guardian, I pledge my fealty to you. I have a score to settle with the new self-proclaimed king of Underhill."* He bowed toward me before settling into a resting position in the grass.

I stared in shock. I just made friends with this magnificent and albeit, terrifying creature. I'd say eat your heart out, but that's a little too close for comfort. *"Well, are you just going to stand there like a deer in the headlights or will you be riding with me."* Alden interrupted my thoughts with his. *"Wait What?"* My mouth dropped. *"Get on guardian, we have a monumental task to undertake. You're wasting time standing there, mouth agape."* With an outstretched hand I walked to him cautiously. I let my fingers glide across his broad neck. His fur felt very much like the moss it resembled. I climbed onto his back. Nervous, I didn't know where to put my hands. It felt only natural to hold onto his backward curving antlers. So, I reached for them hesitantly. They were cold and hard like iron. Alden didn't protest.

Confidence surged through me. *"OK, I can do this. It's like a big fuzzy green Harley, no big deal."* *"DON'T COMPARE ME TO SOME MAN-MADE CONTRAPTION."* Alden's thoughts boomed. *"Wait you heard that...?"* I leaned forward looking at him embarrassed.

"Of course, I did, your mind is very loud. Now I suggest you hold on!" He stood, and before I knew it, we were jettisoned toward the moonlit sky.

Flying above Underhill was exhilarating. I could see Bramblehaven lit up with lanterns on each dwelling. In the distance I could see cities and small towns. Mountains, lakes, swamps, even oceans. One place seemed to call to me like a distant memory, like a song I've heard once before. It had a sense of familiarity to it.

Within the forest, miles from where Alden and I met. There was a swamp alight with bioluminescent mushrooms the size of redwood trees. As I gazed upon it in wonderment, I had the strange sense that it, or something was staring right back at me. I shuddered and turned leaning forward. *"There!"* I shouted to Alden pointing toward Thelgrim's smithy. *"As you wish Guardian!"* Alden echoed as he dove toward the shop.

Underhill truly had its own ecosystem and weather patterns. A world within the world. I don't think I truly believed any of this was real. Until this exact moment, flying between the two parallel plains. The amazement and awe I felt surged through me like lightning crackling through a cloud.

It felt like seconds before we landed outside of Thelgrim's shop. I began to dismount from Alden, patting his neck as a sign of thankful appreciation. My feet on the ground, I turned around to see we were surrounded. Thelgrim, Aluwyn, and Grip came running out startled from the commotion. Their faces however were stricken with a combination of fear and anger. Similar to the face my mother made, when I scared her playing in the street right before she would scold me.

"What were you thinking bringing that-that thing back here!" Aluwyn shouted pointing at Alden. *"Relax, he wants to help."* I tried to reassure them. *"That, thing cannot be trusted! They are bloodthirsty monsters! Ya know what they eat don't ya!"* Thelgrim spoke with fierce agitation. *"It's not what it seems, Here, just look at his shadow!"* Defensive and frustrated I pointed to Alden's silent and constant companion.

The shadow rabbit stood on its hind legs as if it were looking back at us. Its left ear twitched as If it were listening. Before getting back on all fours and hopping about, grazing on the shadows of the grass.

Thelgrim and Aluwyn stared wide eyed in disbelief. Grip, on the other hand, had remained unconvinced. *"Ha, he's probably a terrible hunter and can't catch anything but bunnies."* Grip laughed hysterically, slapping his knees. "Enough." Alden's thoughts boomed and I could tell everyone heard it by their stunned faces. *"I can catch anything with ease. Allow me to demonstrate."* Alden in a show of quickness and agility flipped Grip onto his back with his antlers. The peryton began bucking like a wild bronco sending Grip sprawling through the air into a nearby pile of hay.

Grip emerged with a defiant look in his eyes doing his best to spit strands of hay from his mouth. *"Woah, woah, wait a minute you can speak gryphon toots?"* Aluwyn questioned, shaking off her dazed look. *"My father Creighton taught me."* Alden said, keeping his eyes affixed to Grip. Who was silently mocking him. *"Woah, ya mean to tell me the great Gryphon, Creighton the last king of the forest, The protector of the dryads. The Hero who ended the Goblin Sprite Wars. That Creighton was your father?"* Thelgrim said, running his hand nervously through his hair. *"SINCE MY FATHERS PASSING, I AM THE KING OF THE FOREST!"* Alden's thoughts ablaze with mournful anger. *"Alright, alright I don't mean any offense now."* Thelgrim put his hands up.

"It's almost dawn, we better get a move on." Aluwyn interrupted as she pointed toward the horizon. *"Right, you two come with me to the stables, we will get ourselves a ride."* Thelgrim ushered Grip, and Aluwyn to follow. They were only gone momentarily, but when they returned, I tried as hard as I could to stifle my laughter. Thelgrim astride a Clydesdale. Aluwyn straddled a Kirin and trailing behind them was Grip riding proudly on a goat.

"Laugh it up surfacer!" Grips demeanor changed as he snarled. We set out heading to the west in search of the life tree and the hideout, mounted up and westward bound. It wasn't long till we reached a rocky outcrop, sitting below the mountain range.

Amid the outcrop stood the most magnificent tree I'd ever seen. Each branch held up a different fruit. Its leaves varied in size, shape, and color. It was as if every season was combined into one living plant. Life tree was the perfect name for it because it bore a great array of life. It seemed to glow with a golden sheen. Strong, sturdy, and vibrant.

Alden kneeled to allow my dismount. I headed for the tree, my feet slipping just slightly on the gravel. Getting closer I could see the bark had a familiar softness to it like a cedar, but its color varied like Hawaiian rainbow eucalyptus trees. I knocked 3 times gently onto the tree. The golden light shot from it like a crack in the pavement. It bolted toward a mountain. At the summit a cavern rumbled open.

Peering inside there was a large building made of semi-precious stone. With hexagonal glass domed towers in all four directions, outlining the center buildings arced shaped appearance. Grabbing the golden door knocker, I rapped on the oaken door, and we waited for an answer.

Alden- *The Peryton*

Flight Over Underhill

The Life Tree

The Lost Library

Chapter 6

THE TRAITOR

No answer followed my rapt onto the oaken door, instead it creaked open with an eerie and ancient groan. We stepped inside, our eyes peeled looking for our mysterious friends. The interior of this megalithic building was packed wall to wall with shelves upon shelves of books.

Inches of dust covered almost everything. In the center of the room, were three rectangular tables in a 'u' formation. They were alight with lanterns and candelabras. A magnifying glass with a handle of horn lay next to an open and debris free book.

Though this hidden library was mostly untouched it was obvious someone made this place their home. Two sets of footprints led in every direction. Toward the back of the main room was a hallway. Leading east and west, I assume two separate wings of the building. We glanced at one another quickly. Hearing the distinct sound of footsteps emanating from somewhere down that hall.

"About time you showed up, I began to think the bunch of you were cowards." The gruff voice of the man in blue sounded just before he rounded the corner. He withdrew his hood revealing his face. Cinnamon colored crew cut hair, honey brown eyes, and tanned skin. A faint scar ran into his five o'clock shadow. *"Told you they'd come brother."* The purple cloaked woman's voice sounded as she jumped down from the balcony just above the entrance to the hall. Her cloak curled around her bent legs as she made the landing. Still squatting from her entrance, she flipped her hood back revealing the same Cinnamon colored hair and honey brown eyes. Their features though masculine and feminine were strikingly similar.

"You win this one sister." The man said, scratching at his stubble with a dagger he pulled from the sheath clasped to his leg. *"Welcome to the library."* They said resoundingly. *"This is our best resource; all knowledge is kept here. Scrolls from Alexandria, Timbuktu, Atlantis and even Merlin himself. Not to mention so much more."* The mysterious woman said standing up and walking toward us. *"That lovable brute is Titus."* Nodding her head in her brothers direction. The man still scratching his beard looking uninterested in us. *"And I'm Tilly."* She said with a smile as she offered her hand up to shake. I began to reach for it but was pushed out of the way. As Grip hastily grabbed her hand and began slobbering all over it, with what I assumed was his attempt at a kiss. *"A desert rose never looked so pretty or smelled so sweet."* He bounced his eyebrows in such an awkward manner it reminded me of two caterpillars running away from one another.

Tilly looked down toward her hand and Grip, a mix of confusion and disgust painted on her face. She pulled her hand away. *"Uh, thanks..."* she said trying to shake off the imp's green slime. Titus laughed at this display before warming up to us as he too stepped forward. *"It looks as if we've got our work cut out for us."* He hinted as he cast his gaze toward the bookshelves.

Over the next few weeks, we spent every waking moment studying texts and scrolls. Looking for clues about the clockworks. Reading spells and incantations of every kind from hoodoo to kabbalah, druid to elven. Blending knowledge of both human and fae.

Alden and Titus spent time jousting, dagger to antler. Grip fawned over Tilly every chance he got. Aluwyn would come to her rescue. The two of them, would run off to the farthest reaches of the building and bring back more scrolls and books. I spent my time studying magic and battle strategies. Anything to gain more confidence for the days to come. I decided when it was time to leave here, I'd bring the magnifying glass with me.

Among everything in the library, it fascinated me most. The lens itself had different hinges; each one had a different color magnifier. I discovered that each color could translate a different language. It was probably the greatest fidget toy I had ever seen. I found myself carrying it more and more often. It helped soothe my anxiety. Though I noticed I flipped through the lenses a lot more when talking with Aluwyn. I wonder why that was.

We spent weeks at this library and strengthened not only our knowledge, physical prowess, but also our bond as friends. We discovered our new friends were twins, who ran away from an orphanage in London. They were brought to Underhill by a mysterious fairy, who gave them the clockworks as a gift before pushing them into a fairy ring.

We learned that three of the clockworks never made it to the surface but were stolen from the Dwartin upon completion. The bowl, the sword, and the shield remained somewhere in Underhill. The Dwartin lost track of the thief somewhere, in the Armillaria swamp. We sat down with a map of the swamp and began to discuss, how we should navigate through the mushroom infested area.

It was at that very moment when we were interrupted by a loud crash that echoed through the library. The Glass dome overhead had shattered. It began raining glass down onto us. Shielding ourselves the best we could. We gazed upward. Rappelling down was a team of goblins dressed in black and aiming what looked like electrically charged rifles. Titus quickly flipped one of the tables over, as we huddled for cover behind it.

The oaken door in front of us began to bang. It wasn't long before it came crashing down clearing the room of its dust. A cyclops ducked under the frame and pushed its way in. Emitting an ear shattering roar. Banshees wailed in behind it followed by hellhounds and minotaur. It was an army, and we were trapped like rats.

The room shook as enemies piled in. Our only defense was a rectangular table laying on its side, acting as a shield. My heart pounded. I heard Alden's voice echo in every corner of my mind. *"This is how heroes are born Guardian, we fight!"* Before I could blink or muster up enough courage to look away from the gathering army. I felt Alden's antlers fling me into the air, before landing on his back.

He leapt into the air just as we cleared the table, his wings outstretched, and we began to soar around the room. His head tilted downward as we curved toward the enemy. In one swoop he took out ten goblins, impaling them and throwing them to the wall. As we curved past the front lines. To my right was the weapons wall we set up for our practices. Alden swooped in close enough for me to grab at my weapon of choice, a scimitar.

We began to circle again, as we reached the left side of the room. Alden flew at 180 degrees. He pushed his feet into a gallop on the wall, before pushing off and landing to the floor, head bent. He ran straight for one of the red eyed and pissed off minotaur. He impacted the beast with such a force it flung me back into the air and straight toward the cyclops.

I took my chance and shoved my blade into its massive singular eye with a squelch. Blinded and in a rage, it roared with fury. Just before it grabbed me and threw me toward the large stained-glass window at the back of the library. I heard the glass shatter before I reached it. A loud mechanical **whir** sounded. I collided with something that was not the glass I had expected.

Instead, something caught me like a baseball mitt catching the ball. I slid to my feet and turned. Behind me was a green skinned troll, wearing red pigtails. To her right was a tall and slender cyborg. A closer examination revealed he was also, elven. I caught sight of the clockwork shield as it changed appearance from a mitt, back into its rounded triangular form. The troll smiled at me. The elven cyborg raised his right arm, and a clockwork sword glinted in the new light casting from the broken window.

"Sorry we were late to the party. " He grinned, then yelled *"To arms!"* He shouted charging the horde. *"Ooooooo, I told him I don't wanna do this, he knows I don't like fighting. I'm a pacifist! And I hate ghosts! Here goes nothing, get behind me kid. "* The obviously high-strung troll ranted before she shoved me behind her. *"How does it go again? Oh yeah raaaaaaawwwwwwwrrrrr!"* She bellowed and began to run forward.

Her shield once again morphed, but this time into a large dome as she rushed toward the dwindling army and straight for the cyclops. A metal bang sounded as she managed to hit the cyclops dead on, along with the pack of hellhounds. She pushed them out the door and to the edge of the mountain cliff. They were sent careening down the cliffside. Roars and yelps filled the air.

"I'm Hilda." She said with a toothy grin. *"Now, Let's get back in there, kid."* She grabbed my hand and pulled me behind her. Like a stampede she flew inside the main room. Her broken roar, a mix of anxiety and anguish, halted. It was replaced with a sigh of relief.

"You got rid of them ghosts? Yay!" She began hopping up and down. The room rumbled and a few of the remaining books fell from the now destroyed shelves. *"Of course! I dispatched them immediately; I know you hate those. I've got you covered Hilde."* The elven cyborg gave a charming smile. As he pushed the blonde hair away from in front of his face.

Grip was sitting in a corner trying to catch his breath, sweat beaded on his forehead. Alden stood in the center of the room like a triumphant warrior, his wings twitching restlessly like he wasn't finished. Titus, Tilly and Aluwyn; stood to the right side sheathing their blades.

"Where's Thelgrim?" I asked. Titus and Tilly looked confused. Aluwyn's face contorted with shock. *"We've been here for weeks...how could I have not noticed. We were so busy with studying and practicing...I..I.."* her sentence trailed off, and she hid her tears. *"Come to think of it, I haven't seen him since The Life Tree."* Grip spoke as he stood and sauntered toward us. *"I*

sense there is a Traitor among us." Alden's voice rang into our heads as the room turned their eyes toward him.

"Don't you dare say that! He's like a father to me!" Aluwyn shrilled, her tears overran her face. She tried to conceal them, covering her eyes as she ran down the hall to her quarters. Titus interrupted the still silence that fell after Aluwyn's departure. *"And who might you be?"* He said with an outstretched hand to the Elf. *"I am Finn, and this is my partner, Hilda."* Finn spoke boldly. *"Partners?"* Grip interrupted a puzzled look befell his face as he pointed between the two. *"Why, yes indeed little one!"* Finn chuckled and ruffled grips hair like he was a toddler.

"Do that again and I'll bite your hand off!" Grip snapped. As he tromped away, his skin purplish with embarrassment. Hilda blushed and batted her eyes toward the ground bashfully. *"Aw, you didn't have to tell them!"* She said swiping her foot nervously on the ground. *"Why hide our love, Hilde? After all, is it not pure?"* Finn spoke with compassion.

"Well Because you're just so charmin, and I'm ..." Hilda trailed off. *"Just as beautiful as ever."* Finn assured her with a smile. Before leaning down and kissing her hand. *"Blechh!"* Grip sounded from afar. *"Love is love!"* I called over my shoulder to him.

"You have clockworks too?" I nodded toward the sword and shield. *"Ah, yes curious things but lifesaving. It is quite the story. Tea anyone?"* Finn asked with a smile.

The Twins- *Tilly and Titus*

Finn- Cybernetic Elf

Hilda- Troll

Clockwork Shield

Clockwork Sword

Chapter 7

ARMILLARIA SWAMP

Grip scrambled around the table pouring tea for everyone. Frantically he skidded between cups, before screeching to a halt atop his own chair. It wobbled as he jumped onto it. Finn crossed his right leg over his left, as he picked up his tea with a smirk. He raised his hand to hush the idle chatter. He spoke when it quieted down.

"It was a perfectly normal Sunday; Hilda and I were on our usual afternoon picnic in the Armillaria swamp. Hilda just loves the mushrooms there, isn't that right dear?" Asking with a glance and a charming smile. *"Ooooo yes I do, I do they are so squishy and tasty, and the flavor is to die for!!"* Hilda said, clapping her hands excitingly. *"Yes, I know dear."* Finn followed up as he sipped his tea. *"Well, there we were minding our own business. I had just picked some of her favorite mushrooms, the teal truffle. Just before I began to dice them up for our swamp salad. This phooka ran by in nothing more than a loincloth. Carrying these odd instruments. That's when he dropped the sword and shield. He was in such a rush he never even looked back. He just raised this strange bowl up over his head and kept going. I went over to investigate them and that's when we were attacked by a dragon. I threw Hilda the shield and I took up the sword. We fought it off the best we could. Hilda's shield formed a dome and protected us from the flames. It gave up and flew toward Bramblehaven."* *"That must have been when it attacked us!"* I interrupted. *"Of that I have no doubt, it seems to be hunting these items, Hilda had heard tell of them and suggested we come to the lost library to learn more. That's where we met you."*

"BORING!" Grip shouted, "I've heard better tales from mute mermaids!" He said, spitting into a nearby vase like a spittoon. "He is SOOO rude! That was a lovely story sweetheart!" Hilda said cooing over Finn.

"So, we have a Phooka to find." Alden's voice drifted into our minds. "Yes, but first I think you need to give Aluwyn an apology, we need to work as a team and the less hard feelings the better." I looked at Alden squinting my eyes he had a habit of standing in front of bright lights like the one coming from the now broken stained glass window. "I owe no one an apology! I said what must be spoken!" His voice echoed off my synapses.

"It's ok, I understand that's how it looks. I know Thelgrim, it isn't like him. I believe in my heart of hearts that's true. He can believe what he wants. But my foster father is no Traitor. I have to find him." Aluwyn spoke, wiping tears from her eyes as she appeared around the corner. "Aluwyn you can't go! You have no idea what is going on. You don't even know where he could be." Tilly pleaded with her not to go. "I'm going to find them and no one's stopping me!" She said defensively before turning and flying out the window.

"I'll follow her and make sure she stays out of trouble." Alden's voice rang between our ears again. "Wait Alden you can't go, what if we need you in a fight? You swore your fealty to me, remember?" I spoke boldly. "This is true but if something were to happen to her because of me, I'd be no less of a monster than the rest of my kind. Then my brother." His voice trailed off on the last of his words. I could tell there was pain behind them.

"OK I grant you this, but report back to me in three days so I know you're close by." I gave a gentle nod showing him I understood. He stretched his wings and like a jet plane he took off after Aluwyn. At that moment, Grip jumped down from a bookshelf with a roll of parchment in his hand. *"Well, what are you staring at, we need a plan."* He smiled as he unrolled a map of Armillaria swamp. His tongue lulled out of the corner of his mouth in tune with the concentrated look on his face.

For a moment it was quiet as we watched Grip study the map. He looked up, his blue face turned purple then red with anger. *"Hurry up twinkle toes you were the one to see the phooka last! Why are you just staring at me!"* He shouted towards Finn. Finn jumped in surprise, like he was startled from a daydream and shuffled quickly to the table. *"Right then, we saw it here about the middle it headed west where the mushrooms and trees begin to blend. Over…"* his finger trailed on the map. *"Here!"* He spoke tapping the point on the parchment. *"Alright, looks like we have a treasure hunt on our hand lads."* Titus said with a grin,

"Or a wild goose chase." Grip added *"Phooka's are tricky devils and, talk about annoying with their stinking riddles."* *"Sounds like someone else we know."* I grinned toward Grip. *"Looks to me like you're going to lead this expedition buddy!"* Grips face purple with embarrassment again. I couldn't help but get enjoyment out of it. *"Alright surfacer I'll find your phooka, but only because you can't find your way out of a pint of Centurion Cider."* He snickered, sticking his tongue out at me.

"So, champ, how do we get there, and quickly?" I asked. *"I've got that covered."* Titus rang in, leaning on the table with both hands, a devious smile across his face. A smile that made everyone's stomach turn. *"This can't be good."* I said

ruffling my hair in nervousness. *"Buckle up lads!"* He laughed, before he turned and waved us to follow.

He led us to the back of the library into a dusty and cobweb ridden storeroom. The storeroom must have been located in one of the towers because its ceiling was nowhere in sight... In the center was a rickety wooden spiral staircase. I began to feel queasy as I noticed Titus began to climb them. Beckoning once again to the rest of us to follow. It was a long way up. The few times I caught myself looking down, I held back vomit.

It wasn't that I was afraid of heights. I was afraid of falling and these stairs were in no way maintained. They squeaked and cracked when stepped on. Some were missing. A handful of times we had to leap gaps where two or three steps should have been. At one point Hilda who was at the back stepped on a plank, and it broke causing her to slip.

"I'm gonna die!" She shouted as her balance faltered, beginning to fall backward. Finn quickly spun around and caught her hand pulling her to safety. *"The only falling you'll do is for me."* He declared pulling her toward him. *"As if I wasn't sick enough!"* Grip uttered, pretending to gag. The two love birds brushed themselves off, before beginning their ascent after us.

We had reached the top. Titus pushed open a hatch door leading us out. Surprisingly the exit led to the top of the mountain that hid the library. We clambered out onto its peak. Titus stood in a triumphant manner, his fists on his hips, elbows out. He faced the rest of us and just when I thought it couldn't get worse, he took a sidestep revealing three rickety old coal carts latched together.

Like a terrifying abandoned roller coaster ride. It sat upon a rusted track that seemed to go on for miles down the mountain with twists and turns. Hanging from cliff sides. It went from one side of the mountain to the other, and back again. Before finally vanishing into the forest below.

"Well lads ya can't really buckle up, but ya better hold on tight." Titus smirked. *"Nope, no way, I'm not dying today."* *"Awe, grippy just for me?"* Tilly said, giving him a peck on the cheek. Grip's face turned pink.

"Well now, that's a new shade." I thought to myself. A Surge of confidence swelled through him as he began orating. *"You heard him you scaredy kitties let's go! Let's go!"* He went to the back of the line pushing on Hilda and Finn who hardly budged at his shoves. We all began to laugh in an uproar.

Our laughs quickly subsided as a low rumble began to replace it. *"ROCKSLIDE! GO, GO, LET'S MOVE!!"* Titus shouted. Guiding us one after the other into the carts, before he gave them a shove and jumped in.

The cart jolted and began careening down the mountainside. Every twist and turn felt like it might have flung us overboard. Trees and mountain goats flashed by us, in nothing more than a blur. We all screamed just before the forest's threshold. Tree limbs smacked at us. Grip spat out a mouthful of leaves. Bugs splatted in our faces. *"I don't like this one bit!"* Hilda yelled from the front cart as she stomped her feet. They crashed through the bottom of the boxcar. Sending the makeshift train into an abrupt halt. We all went flying through the air landing with a thud onto the forest floor.

Titus laughed *"I told you I'd get us here quick. Everyone alright then?"* A chorus of pained yeses swept the air. *"Get me down from here!"* Grips' voice sounded. We looked up to see him dangling on a tree limb from his midsection, seven feet from the ground. Hilda with little effort reached up and snapped the branch, and Grip collided with the ground knocking the breath out of him. *"I deserved that..."* Grip coughed out.

Looking up I saw the swamp. The tree sized bioluminescent mushrooms, growing around bubbling greenish-brown waters. Mosquitos the size of hawks flew in zigzagged patterns over the muck. *"Gross, Grip, did you crap yourself?"* I said holding my nose and wafting the air away. The smell was acrid. An unholy stench comparable to a cross between carrion and an outhouse.

"Shut up surfacer, that wasn't me, it's the swamp." He fired back, getting to his feet. In the corner of the swamp was a moss-covered shack. Its stone chimney crumbled at the top. Boards along the wall were curling due to water damage. *"Cue the banjos."* I muttered *"You, are an odd fellow."* Finn shook his head at me. *"Well, shall we meet our host for tonight's occasion?"* He followed up.

We came to the door, I was about to knock, when it flew open, and the strangest creature I had ever laid eyes on, stood before me. Its red skin had a leather like appearance. Its face was similar to a goblin but, had a slight beak to it. Atop its head was a pair of rabbit ears, and the horns of a goat. Long shaggy and matted white hair went down his back, stopping just before his loincloth. A fox tail flicked to and fro behind him. Its eyes were big and round, similar to a lemur.

   "Nice to meet I!" it said putting out its hand. *"Uh, nice to meet you?"* I grimaced. A wave of confusion swept over me. *"That's what me say, don stay out."* I stood there just staring, not sure exactly what to do. *"Surfacer, he means come in."* Grip said, pushing past me. *"Me make soup; you eat?"* He ladled soup from a cauldron into some stone bowls and passed them around. *"Thanks, I think. We came because we were..."* *"Shh! Shh! eat, eat ask I later, eat."* The phooka interrupted me.

   Almost in unison we lifted our bowls, starving we drank the soup in gulps. Finishing off the soup my stomach lurched, and I wasn't feeling very well. Looking around, I could tell everyone else was feeling ill as well. *"What...what...did you do?"* I muttered as the stone bowl fell from my hand.

Iniko-*Phooka*

Chapter 8

THE TRICKSTER

"Here us go!" The phooka exclaimed, dancing about in circles making odd faces at everyone. He put his hands on either side of his head. Touching his thumbs to his temples he waved his hands back and forth. Making odd ululating noises and blowing raspberries.

The colors in the room began to shift. The brown hut changed before my eyes, into blue then green, followed by reds, and purples. The air surrounding my skin seemed to vibrate. I looked around, Tilly was laughing uncontrollably in the corner at Titus, who was trying to touch his fingers together but somehow managed to keep missing.

I looked toward Grip his eyes began to shift in size. First the left and the right, his face warping. The walls began to melt away and, ceased to exist altogether. We were somewhere in between nothing and everything all at once.

Hilda and Finn sat together. They were sitting on the ground, picking invisible flowers taking turns smelling their vacant scents. Smiling at one another with idle chatter.

Grip joined the phooka in dancing around. The longer I stared, the longer they began to resemble orangutans chasing one another.

My heart felt like a drum. It pitter-pattered and began to flutter like a butterfly. I looked out the window that had appeared, in the vast and white emptiness.

I saw the blue glowing mushrooms, accompanied by a symphony of fireflies. Flashing their green lights brightly, to light up the night.

Slowly as I gazed outward, I began to relate to those little fireflies, so tiny and surrounded by darkness. Why, they didn't feel overwhelmed at all; they just did their very best to light up the night communicating with their friends and family. It was their togetherness that lit up the night.

That's it! An epiphany struck me. That's how we could save Underhill! If we do this together, we can be heroes. Just like that, it was as if someone pulled a drain stop from a sink and my surroundings whirlpooled from the strange and abnormal, back into an assemblance of normalcy.

My eyes stung. I felt groggy like I had just woken up from a dream. Though I was almost certain I hadn't been dreaming or asleep for that matter. When my hazy vision cleared, I had a sudden realization. We were no longer inside the phooka's hut. Instead, we were all piled lazily on its porch staring back at the front door, but where was the phooka?

"What happened, where did he go?" I groaned, reaching for my head as a sharp pain made itself known. *"That's a phooka for ya, playing tricks. Picking up strangers bringing em on wild and terrifying rides before dropping em' back off where they started. Stinking phooka's!"* Grip growled, wiping drool from his bottom lip, shaking off his wariness. *"He must have given us a sampling of stupor soup. A sort of potion if you will."* Finn yawned, stretching his arms pulling Hilda closer to him.

"That was a bloody good time if ya ask me!" Titus laughed as he stood up arching his back. He brushed the dirt from his knees. *"Only because you had a babysitter the whole time, you could barely walk!"* Tilly giggled, giving her brother a light shove.

I stood up last, trying to gather my wits. *"Well, shall we?"* I asked looking to the others. They nodded in unison as I reached out my hand to knock. The door flew open before it made contact, it startled me again. There, was the phooka staring at me with its big round eyes. *"Nice to meet I!"* It said putting out its hand. *"Uh, nice to meet you?!"* I furrowed my brow. A new wave of confusion passed over me. *"That's what me say, don stay out."* I stood there just staring, not sure exactly what was going on. Was I having some weird sort of Deja-vu. *"Come on!"* Grip said, pushing me inside. *"Me make soup; you eat?"* He ladled soup from a cauldron into some stone bowls and passed them around. *"Um, no thanks, we came because we were..."* *"Shh! Shh! eat, eat ask I later, eat."* The phooka interrupted me.

Everyone except Titus put down their bowls, Tilly elbowed Titus in the gut. Mouthing the word 'no' and pointing from him to the table. Indicating he set the bowl down as well. Titus rolled his eyes and reluctantly put the bowl down but, not before stealing a drop on his finger and giving it a taste. *"Not this time, no tricks. We came because you were seen running through the swamp with a Clockwork bowl and those..."* I asserted designating toward the sword and shield.

The Phooka's eyes darted unblinkingly between me and the items. A long pause before it spoke. *"Me don't know what you're talking about."* The phooka nodded its head smiling. *"Yes, you do!"* I replied with intensity, shaking my finger at him like a scolding parent.

"Aaaiieeeee!!" the phooka exclaimed, throwing its hands over its head, huddling. *"Me steal em, me steal em, from funny faced man with square mustache! You no spy, are you?*

You don't hurt poor Iniko? Yes?" Iniko groveled. Grabbing my hands as if asking for forgiveness. "No, I won't hurt you Iniko, I need your help" I said, patting his shoulder.

      "Yes! Yes! I help, I help. Me have magic bowl! Magic bowl make Potions! Ookie, spooky, potions from nothing. Just think to make. Fancy bowl! Magic bowl! Mustache man no have any clue what hit him!" He began dancing around the room excitedly. *"Me have special trick too! You, see? Boo!"* Before my eyes Iniko changed his form and I stared back at my reflection, however I don't remember having rabbit ears on top of my head. *"Me you, you, see? Good fun! good fun!!"* Iniko spoke eagerly, hopping in circles clapping his hands with excitement. His claps ended abruptly, and he rushed to hide under a table, as a voice rang through the air.

      "GAURDIAN, GAURDIAN WHERE ARE YOU?" Alden's voice reverberated my brain so much it rang in my ears. *"Somethings wrong!"* I shouted running out the front door. Alden crashed to the ground. I ran toward him crouching beneath his wing. I pushed him to his feet. He stood shaking, covered in scratches and bite wounds. His blood dripped to the ground. Alden's eyes winced in pain with every step we took. *"Help me! He's hurt badly, we must get him inside."* I pleaded with the others as they came to my aide. We hoisted him inside the phooka's shack, where Alden collapsed.

      Alden was unconscious, his breathing was labored. I flew, in uncontrollable grief to Iniko's wash basin. I scrambled blindly as tears began to flood my eyes. I clawed the clockwork flower from my pocket, distraught. I couldn't, no, wouldn't lose my friend. I plunged the clockwork flower into the water. Green and gold streaming light burst out of the flower just as it had in the meadow with Aluwyn.

It had brought the beastly bug back to life, it could heal my friend. I watched as the light streams flowed forth and danced about the room. They came nowhere near Alden, but instead flowed out of the windows and under the loose hanging door. Completely avoiding my dying friend. *"No come back!"* I shouted attempting to command the lights. *"No, no. No work, not dead! Only dying."* Iniko said, clicking his tongue with a worried glance to his window. *"Me fix, me fix."* he said ruffling Alden's fur. *"You fix big, big mess you make out the inside."* He said wide eyed pointing to the door *"Big mess?"* I sniffled wiping my nose. *"What big mess?"* *"You resurrect dead."* He said unblinkingly before continuing. *"In big swamp, that no good news."* He paused again as if in thought. *"Big swamp.... is big dead thing."*

I stood there awestruck as I watched Iniko grab the clockwork bowl. He put a cap on top of the mechanism, as he began to shake it rapidly. Muttering to himself *"Heal friend, Heal friend."* He pried the lid off of it. Red smoke began pouring out of the empty bowl, enveloping Alden.

Iniko looked up at me and panicked. He began jumping up and down and pointing to the door. *"Go fix! Go fix!"* My mind clicked into focus, and I ran out the door, the others close behind. That's when I realized the severity of my mistake. The swamp began to come alive! Dead trees blossomed, the once muck filled waters clean and renewed, but in the midst of the new life, boney and flesh melted hands raised out of the soil. Hundreds of them, like blooming flowers. Simultaneously they began pulling themselves out of the dirt and grime. *"Why is this happening? The Ladyvine didn't look like this!"* *"To put it simply my dear fellow, decay. These gents have been dead for some time, and something tells me they preferred it."* Finn spoke boldly pointing the clockwork sword toward the apocalyptic scene.

He cocked the hilt of the sword, and it ignited the blade with a white-hot flame. I looked onward into the faces of the skeletal and zombie remains of Trolls, and Bog Hags. Then came the Vodyanoy, Shi Shiga, Rougarou, and Kappa. All of them covered in black muck. The ground rumbled and quaked. I feared something much worse was to follow. I was right.

Nine monstrous heads grew like trees from the ground. There long necks intertwined joining at the base of one enormous body. *"It's a, it's a... HYDRA!!!"* Fear choked at my throat. I remembered the stories my mom would tell me about this horrific beast, almost impossible to slay. *"What have you done?"* Tilly called. Titus answered in my stead. *"He started the party!"* A malicious grin stretched on his face. *"Now let's have some fun, shall we?"* With that, we readied our weapons and began tearing through the now forgotten swamp. Each of us, dispatching the heads of the creatures before us.

"I need a hand here!" Grip called. I looked toward his voice, and saw he was being held up by two giant slimy hands of a Vodyanoy. It's Frog like mouth open wide ready to swallow Grip whole. I launched myself from rock to rock. *"Help!"* Grip shouted. Every second that passed he grew closer to becoming an Hors D'oeuvre. Just when the sole of grips shoe touched the Vodyanoy's outstretched lip, my scimitar came down slicing its

arm like butter. Grip managed to get loose as the Vodyanoy squealed with pain. One last swipe of my blade ended its misery.

I looked past the field of now charred and broken bones, to see everyone gathered under the dome of Hilda's shield. Two of its heads were missing, cauterized by Finn's blade. However, the enraged hydra had begun a furious onslaught. Two heads slammed at the shield like ax blades attempting to chop a tree to the ground. The other three shot lightning, fire, and noxious gas at the shield. The last head reached to the sky, with a shrill and continuous roar.

I watched in horror as my friends were pushed further backward. A wooden slam sounded from behind me. I glanced over my shoulder. On the porch of Iniko's humbled shack, stood Alden. *"I'm back guardian, and I'm hungry!"* His thoughts boomed. He galloped faster and stronger than ever, across the messy wetland straight for Hilda's domed shield. Using it like a ramp, he launched through the air and shot through the hydra's chest, to the other side. Leaving a Cervidae sized hole that blasted clean through the hydra. It slumped over, leaving Alden in plain sight. Covered in blood feasting on its heart. Grip turned green and covered his mouth. Regaining his composure, *"That's disgusting! Do you know how long that thing has been dead for?"* He yelled toward Alden. Alden slurped at the last of the heart and turned back. *"I'm sorry, did you want some?"* Grip couldn't hold back and let loose the contents of his stomach onto the ground.

Clockwork Bowl

Chapter 9

THE RESCUE PLAN

We all gathered inside Iniko's hut. After cleaning up the aftermath. We sat around the small Woodfire. Alden stood before us. He had news, and I'll admit we were all curious as to what happened to him.

"I followed Aluwyn as far as Telmara, just as soon as we patched things up. We fell into a bit of trouble. I insisted we just patrol the area, Aluwyn however needed proof of Thelgrim's innocence." Alden shook his head.

"She flew too close to the dark palace. Peering in its clouded windows. She was discovered and it was too late. We were swarmed in seconds. Harpies by the hundreds encircled us, tearing at us with their claws. Aluwyn and I fought them off. Knocking them from the sky. One by one, they fell like drops of rain. In the heart of the battle, I was lost in the fight, when I heard her calling out for me." He paused, looking at the floor scuffing it with his hoof. *"I turned to see her dragged inside. At that same moment the harpies struck me from the sky. I fell into the river. I woke up, hours later and heard her cries. I followed them to the west tower. She has been locked up in there, but she is still very much alive, for now. I fear we are running out of time to save her."* Alden finished.

"Out of the frying pan, and into the fire." Titus chimed in standing up from his seat. *"Let's go!"* He announced. *"It's not that easy killer, we've gotta make a plan or we all die."* Tilly reasoned. *"We're not ready if you ask me!"* Grip spoke with contempt. *"Not so hard. Me break in all da time, good food, good food for Iniko."* The phooka grinned. *"But how do you do it Iniko?"* I asked him for an explanation. The next hour was a

blur as Iniko did his best to explain. Between his broken wording, and a game of charades. We finally had our plan.

"We're dead, we're dead, that's it. There is no way this is going to work!" Grips ever ceasing optimism failed to astound us. "It really is a good plan." Tilly spoke up. "Yeah, give the tyke a chance. Let him prove his worth." Titus added. "You'll see, he may be a trickster, but that's his strength not his downfall." I consoled Grip with a pat on his back. Grip's face was painted with the words 'not amused' written all over it.

"I'm in!" I put my hand to the center of the group. Tilly walked across the room next and, put her hand on mine. "I'm all in". "I never turn down a fight"! Titus smiled adding his hand. "Of course, I am. After all, what are friends for"? Finn smiled and added to the pile. Hilda's voice chimed in. "You can count on me to help save that poor lil firefly". "I swore my fealty to you, Ari, and I owe it to her". Alden placed his hoof gently on the stack. We all looked to Grip with silent stares. "Alright, alright I'll go, but I still don't think it's going to work." He hopped down from a box and finished the union.

We shifted our gaze to Iniko. "Lead the way." I smiled. "Yaaaay! me go, me get to help! Me show you for certain, me you friend!" Iniko burst with excitement. Dancing about the room. Iniko pushed the table aside and underneath was a trap door. He explained earlier that he knew a cave system that led to Telmara. We could take it to stay undetected. He failed to mention however, it was right under our noses, and he had dug it himself. With heavy sighs, we climbed down the ladder and into the caves. The trap door shut. It was so dark inside, that I couldn't see the hand I held in front of my face. "See! Doomed *just like I said!"* Grip announced. *"Wait, wait, me fix, me fix. Hush, hush grumps!"* I could hear him fastening the lid to the Clockwork bowl. Shaking it, he spoke.

"Bright and shiny, bright and shiny. Need a light for me to see."

With a ***whir*** and a ***click,*** the lid popped upward from the bowl. A cylinder of light held the lid in place, quite similarly to an antique lantern. Iniko took advantage of the newfound light and blew raspberries at Grip.

"You two fight like siblings!" I said shaking my head, laughing. We started down the cave system. Iniko led the way. Something told me this wasn't going to be a leisurely walk.

We made our way through the dark winding tunnels. They were about as scattered, as Iniko's speech patterns. I felt at home in the tunnels though. They reminded me of how my brain can go off track. Pondering this and that, while I got lost in thought for a while. Relating one subject to another, and so on. Until I've ended up very far away from where I started. In fact, that, was where we were at this exact moment, very far into the snaking darkness.

The light casting from Iniko's Clockwork bowl made our shadows dance along the cavern walls. Was it me, or were the shadows beginning to dissipate? They vanished altogether, as our tunnel turned into a cliffside path, overlooking a cavernous opening.

A few spots in its rocky rooftop, let light in. Giving it a faint blue glow. Looking down to its depths from our narrow path, I could see scorched and gnawed bones. *"This must be the dragon's home..."* I whispered to myself. Iniko's ears twitched at the sound of my voice. *"Yes, yes dragon sleep here at night. Must keep moving. Me no want to be snack for sulfur breath. Almost there. Hold your centaurs."* Iniko waved us forward on the narrowing pathway.

I heard some rock begin to give way and **clatter** to the ground. It echoed through the cave. I brought my gaze back to the path ahead. There was an opening in the rock face, just down the confined trail. A dim yellow light made our destination evident. Down below, there was a much larger opening in the rock wall, but it looked dark and uninviting.

The walls and pathway began to **rumble**. I hadn't noticed but the light of the cavern had faded away. Iniko spun around, almost slipping. He pressed a finger to my lips and held one to his. A pensive and wide-eyed stare washed over his face.

" Shh-shh. We need be quiet now. Very much quiet. Dragon come home." "Oh, give me a break you can't expect us *to believe...."* Grips protests were interrupted, by a loud **roar** and a puff of flames coming from the dark entryway below us. Powerful thundering footsteps seemed to emanate all around us. We were all stopped dead in our tracks, eyes locked on the scene a hundred feet below.

Emerging from the dark, the dragon that still haunted my dreams since its first attack, Sauntered in. Flames licked from its nostrils. It swayed wearily, tired from its day of hunting no doubt. Its heavy feet *crunched* on bones, while it made its way toward the other side of the cavern. As it passed. We began to sidestep ever closer to our destination. Keeping our eyes on the threat below. It began to turn and coil around itself like a cat about to nap.

Grips footing slipped and some loose gravel fell. A heart attack in every echoed thud, as we stifled our screams. The dragon's eyes shot open, and it saw us. Its head raised and its mouth began to glow. It shot an inferno straight for us as we dove inside. Just barely making it into the small lit cavern. The flames acted as a doorway and shut behind us.

The tired dragon let out a dissatisfied grumble. Its interest lost, with an already full stomach the dragon curled back up to sleep. As we made our way up the ladder to the surface. Telmara at last, we had arrived. This huge fae city was once a thriving metropolis. Now it was nothing more than a policed necropolis. We entered the city in a dark alleyway.

Though much of the city was dark. It reminded me of the time mom, and I had lived in Las Vegas, before we moved to Manhattan. If Las Vegas were a blend of technology and magic, science and the arcane.

It was lit up with holographic billboards, neon lights and bioluminescent plants. A blend of industry and forest. Vines crawled up the sides of tech covered buildings. Ferns broke through concrete slabs. We sat in the alley and surveyed. Fairies, and pixies begged passing goblins for Spice and Soma. Offering what little they had, mostly themselves.

Though the city once thrived, most of the locals looked to be in poverty. The ones who didn't, were militarized. They were easy to spot, like mindless zombies. They all had on that strange metal collar with the telltale blue light. The very same collar as the dragon, and the horde that attacked us wore in the library.

The patrols here were tight and especially dangerous. There were of course goblin units like the ones we had seen before, but they mostly acted as police for the citizens. What was worse was the militarized units of Redcaps. Marching up and down the streets with long pikes in their hands. Their caps and beards were stained with the blood of their victims.

They were one of the few I read about in my book *"Faeries, Fae, and Magical Beings."* The same book that helped me unlock the clockwork flower. I remember it said that Redcaps were homicidal Fae, that they had an insatiable bloodlust. Redcap's favorite activities were to hunt and kill without mercy.

If they weren't bad enough marching the streets. We had to worry about the air patrols of harpies gazing downward like starving vultures. Now, we just had to make it through the city undetected, and I think that is going to be a problem. Our only chance was Iniko's plan. I just hope he knows what he is doing, or we are all going to end up dead.

Chapter 10

THE REVEALING RESCUE

It was now or never. We had to get to the tower and save Aluwyn. A chilling **roar** filled the air. That was our Cue. We turned our heads upwards to see Alden flying straight for the harpies.

"You didn't think I'd give up that easily, did you? You half-witted harbingers. I've come for a real fight!" He projected his thoughts loud and clear. Right, the diversion landed perfectly, while the harpies were busy, and the city's onlookers kept a watchful eye to the skies. It was Grip's turn.

He pulled out a satchel of goblin steel handcuffs. The same type he used on me when we first met. Each of us placed them on our wrist and were bound to one another with chains. While Iniko remained free, the wild card.

This was it; He was up. *"This is your time to shine Iniko."* I said in hushed tones. *"Yes, yes I help, I good friend, you watch, brrrrrrrriiiiiiiiii"!* He began to shake and crack as his form shifted. He grew taller, his shadow cast down onto me. With a snap and a pop his transformation was complete. Standing before me was the epitome of wickedness in all of humankind. Once feared on earth before my time. The wicked man who began the hostile takeover of Underhill.

Adolf, an exact replica, except for the rabbit ears atop his head. *"You really can't do anything about those ears?"* Grip challenged rolling his eyes with a huff. *"Sorry me no perfect stink breath!"* Iniko argued and swiftly grabbed the lead. As he took his place in front. We noticed he had not one, but two flaws in his disguise. Out of the back of his military uniform, Iniko's foxtail flourished. I clapped my hand to my forehead. *"Oooo it's a good thing goblins and redcaps are dumb!"* Hilda blushed trying not to laugh. He paraded us through the streets toward the tower.

Every now and then I tilted my downward turned head and I'd catch a glimpse of a watchful eye. They had to know, they had to. To my surprise no one stopped us or questioned anything. Iniko kept on marching. Before long we reached the front gates of the citadel that housed the tower. It was guarded on either side by two armor-clad and very beefy minotaur. They hadn't noticed us, as they were watching the battle above.

I followed their gaze. Alden was holding his own against the harpies. At that moment, he knocked another one from the sky. It came careening downward with a splat on the concrete. Landing between the bullheaded guards and the imperfect Adolf clone. *"Password?"* The guard to the left, spoke promptly with a snort. *"Oh, you can't be serious Marty, it's the boss, you can't ask the boss for the password."* The minotaur to the right said whimsically. *"Oh, come on. I stand here all day and never get to say it!"* The huskier guard whined. *"Oh fine, if you must, but don't blame me if he cuts off your head."* The melodic minotaur stood back at attention, trying hard to avert his eyes from the situation. With a snort, the deep voice guard retracted his statement.

"Right, sorry boss. Go right in." He shrugged toward the entrance. The large gates opened, and Iniko pulled us inside. It was dark and very poorly lit. Tattered curtains hung off railings and stained-glass windows, wafting in the cold echoed draft. "It's empty." I said aloud. *"All except for me, surfacer swine."* A tiny Bogart dressed like a butler said, in a high pitched but gruff voice. *"And you? What are you doing out of your cell?*

I didn't know the boss let you out?" He said looking directly at Iniko. *"Me am, boss man!"* Iniko's voice came from Adolf's mouth. *"Ohh really, I'll just have to tell the boss you think so!"* The bogart butler turned around to walk away.

With a quickness, Iniko snatched him up in the clockwork bowl. *"Hey! Let me out of here. You're going to regret this! When I tell the boss he will eat you! Let me out!"* The butler's tiny fist banged from inside of the bowl. Iniko frantically shook the bowl, muttering. *"Friend, friend, till the end."* *"Woaaahhh, hey stop it out there I'm gonna be sick!"* The bogart yelled. Iniko kept shaking the bowl. *"Friend, friend, till the end, friend, friend, till the end!"* The banging and hollering stopped, and the room fell silent.

Iniko tilted the bowl to the floor and unclasped the lid. Pink smoke creeped across the floor like dry ice. A very small and much more pleasant looking figure emerged. He had turned the bogart into a brownie. The sharply dressed butler, had also now donned a top hat. *"Buford is the name friends, right this way!"*

The tiny butler began to lead us up the tattered carpeted staircase. Having to do pull-ups on every step. We were ever closer to Aluwyn and her freedom. But at this rate it would take forever. I scooped up Buford and placed him onto my shoulder. *"Lead the way little man"* I grinned. Buford pointed upwards as the staircase climbed. *"Be there soon, Aluwyn."* I thought to myself.

The stairs seemed to wind on forever. As we climbed higher and higher up the holding tower of the citadel. It felt as if the winding stairway would never cease. It was then when we came to an abrupt stop.

There was a large metal door separating the rest of the tower from where we stood. Reaching out quietly trying to make as little sound as possible, I tried to push the latch down with my thumb and open the door. It wouldn't budge, the latch was stuck fast, it was locked. *"I don't suppose you have the key?"* I said looking to my right shoulder at Buford, who seemed to be as pleased as punch with the ride up. *"Why no, my friend, only the master of the house is the keeper of the key."* Buford replied shaking his head vigorously. Causing his top hat to slide around on his head. *"He's not the only one, step aside lads. Have it open in a jiff."* Titus announced as he pushed his way to the front.

"Clockwork key, Open the door in front of me, tis passage I seek."

He whispered to his Clockwork and kissed it for luck; it began to **whir** and **sputter**. The teeth began shifting and changing. It stopped with a **click**. He pushed it into the hole above the latch and gave it a turn. The door gave way as it **creaked** open, and the noise grew louder.

It revealed a nightmarish scene. Lining the twisting staircase were rows and rows of holding cells. Within each were creatures from every walk of life. From Scarecrow esq. Bubaks, To devilish wendigo. Sprites and elves. Centaurs and Chupacabra's paced their small spaces. Even creatures I'd never seen or heard of and, they were all screaming to be let out, to be free.

"Damn, go on I'll catch up. I can't leave them here." Titus remarked. *"What are you talking about Titus? We need you; you have the key!"* My heart pounded a mix of fear and worry. *"It seems to me old rough and rugged has a heart, grant him this Ari."* Finn smirked softly. *"Go on I said! Tilly is the best lock picker I know, you're in good hands. Now go!"* He put an end to the conversation as he began opening the cells.

He was right, with the door open there was no doubt the whole city knew something was up. The cacophony of screams could wake the dead. We quickened our pace. *"ALMOST THERE!"* I yelled trying to get my message over the ambiance. My steps slowed and came to a stop. I lost control of myself. My gaze cast to the cell on my left. I was being pulled in. A siren called to me from her gilded cage. She was floating in an abnormally sized fish tank at its center.

"Come to me, set me free, yours I'll be, you'll belong to me."

Her voice echoed the halls pulling Finn and Grip in, we began to press our faces to her cell like zombies. *"Oooo we ain't got time for this! Back off fish lips!"* Hilda shouted stampeding toward us. Just like that she picked all three of us up and slung us over her shoulder, stomping up the stairs glaring at Finn. When our hypnotic state died down, I caught a glimpse of the siren, who was now hissing at us baring rows of shark like teeth, I shuddered. Hilda tossed us down onto the platform.

We had reached the top. Scrambling to our feet I looked around. There were only 3 cells on this platform. Quickly I ran to the first one. It sat empty with only a pool of dried blood by its door. My heart raced. *"We can't be too late, we can't."* I thought to myself. I rushed to the next cell. A disheveled man in a military uniform sat on the floor holding his head. A collar on his neck like those we've seen before. I halted here baffled. He looked up at me with a crazed look in his eyes.

A small square mustache sat on his lip. *"Adolf?"* I asked quizzically. The man's eyes glazed over, and he began rocking back and forth ***laughing maniacally***. Confusion was cast over me. *"What is going on?"* I whispered.

"Ari, Ari is that you?" A familiar voice rang through the air. I ran to the last cell. It was Aluwyn, she was alive. *"Tilly I've found her, get her out of here!"* I yelled over my shoulder. Tilly ran over and began working away.

"Why are you guys here! You shouldn't have come. He will kill you. Just like he, he, he...." She began to sob. *"Aluwyn, what's going on?"* I asked. Reaching through the cell, placing a hand on her shoulder. Slowly she raised her head. *"Just like he killed Thelgrim."* She lost herself crying hysterically.

Tilly fumbled with the lock. As we all bowed our heads, feeling her pain. We lost a friend. What was there to say. *"You know, my dear boy, you should listen to the stupid girl."* A sinister chill ran through my blood. This new voice echoed in my head. It was cold and unpleasant. The kind of voice that belonged to someone twisted and deranged.

"Oh no!" Aluwyn shouted, scrambling to the farthest wall of her cell; she huddled down and buried her face into her knees. We turned around to find a face to match the unfamiliar voice. My downward turned head, caught a glimpse of a dwarven shadow on the floor. Almost with a life of its own, it

waved at me like it knew me. I followed the shadow to its keeper. That's when I saw it wasn't a dwarf at all, but something much more terrifying.

"*Aliester...*" I whispered. "*Clever boy, now, tell me how a delectable morsel like yourself, knows my name?*" The beast chortled with malice. His mouth foamed and dripped with slobber. I never felt fear so much, that I actually tasted its shocking bitterness. Until his red crazed eyes met mine.

The hairs on my body stood on end and felt like the pinpoints of acupuncture. This time my heart didn't race. It jumped from my chest, leaving me choking on the air around the room.

***

Buford- Bogart Form

Buford- *Brownie Form*

Clockwork Bangle

Chapter 11

THE BURNING PYRE

Dread filled the room, like a thick fog you could cut with a knife. Unlike Alden this peryton was much more like those of Mythological lore. He was the epitome of twisted and depraved. He gave off the same sinister vibe a serial killer would, in an interview. His eyes were wild and looked through you like you weren't even there. His mad, and sinister grin dripping with rabid foam, ceased in an instant. He lifted his head and his psychotic gaze moved to the wall behind me.

At that precise moment the stone wall crashed inward. Debris filled the air. When the dust cleared Alden stood in the doorway he created. *"Guardian! Get behind me! ALL OF YOU NOW!"* His inner voice rang through our heads. As he inserted himself between us and Aliester. *"Oh, I see now."* Aliester said. A hostile grin set on his beak. *"Dear brother, how far you've fallen hanging out with the rabble and filth. I recall dear old mum telling us not to play with our food."* He shot a mad glance toward Alden. *"None have fallen as far as you little brother."* Alden shot back a look of hatred I'd never seen come out of him before

"Ah, tsk-tsk. You may have taken our father's place as king of the forest. But I, my dear brother, have built my own throne and soon will rule over everything!" Aliester's' laughter echoed sickeningly through our consciousness. *"Don't you dare speak of father!"* Alden lowered his head ready to charge. *"Oh, you're not still mad, are you? After all it was such a long time ago."* Aliester's face grew even darker in his own madness as he whispered menacingly. *"Since I ate his heart out!"* Aliester's laughter echoed again.

"I'll kill you!" Alden's voice reverberated so loud it caused my vision to blur. *"I am afraid, that will have to wait my friend."* Finn rested a hand on Alden's shoulder. *"Seems Titus, finished his self-proclaimed mission."* Finn nodded in Aliester's direction. As the streets outside began clamoring with the shouts of freedom and reckless abandon.

"What is that wretched sound?" Aliester's head turned toward the wall behind him. *"That would be the sound of freedom. Your army escaped before you could brainwash them."* Finn smiled and gave a nod. *"No!! You fools! What have you done! Well, no matter, with this trinket I'll soon have them back."* Aliester gloated. He lifted his right cloven foreleg and gave it a boastful shake. That's when I saw it wrapped snugly around the shank of his leg. The clockwork bangle. The only clockwork we had yet to recover was in the hands of the enemy.

Aliester gave a sinister chuckle, his leg still raised. As a whir sounded and the side of the bangle opened. Revealing a gun barrel. Sparks flew from it as it shot a coil of metal toward me. Alden hit the coiled object from the air with his antlers. It slapped to the ground and slid across the floor stopping a few feet from me. A coiled flimsy mass of metal, with a blinking square blue light lay still on the floor. In our distraction. Aliester pushed past us with a quickness similar to Alden's. Shouldering a passing cell door, releasing Adolf.

Adolf clung to Aliester as They flew out of the hole in the wall. Finn stepped out in front and faced us. *"Now is the time for action my friends. We can slip out of the city undetected while the guards are distracted with the recent prison break.*

Now, it is the matter of our next move that is vital, where to?" He looked at me as did everyone.

My mind was blank, and I didn't have an answer. There was too much pressure. I began to say *"Well I, I suppose we should..."* *"Ari..."* Aluwyn's voice sounded meek. I ran to her. I placed my hands on her shoulders. She looked up at me with tears in her eyes. Her arms wrapped around her waist like She was trying to hold herself together. *"Ari, I want to go home..."* Her head bowed on the last word like the weight of the world was coming down on her. I knew what had to be done. I looked back toward Finn and announced, *"We will go to Bramblehaven and recover. Split up! Alden, Buford, and I will take Aluwyn to ensure her safety. Finn, you take Hilda, Tilly, and Titus. Retrieve what you can from the lost library and meet us in Bramblehaven. Grip, you, and Iniko are going to have to learn how to get along and get out of Telmara together. Give them hell as you go. Take their defenses down a notch."* *"Yes-yes, they no, no what hit them!"* Iniko grinned morphing into a rabbit eared Grip. *"Don't do that!"* Grip *protested.*

"It's about time I gotta have a little fun!" Grip said, spinning the daggers from his belt. *"It's settled then, we will meet at Thelgrim's shop."* The last words hung in the air; sadness filled me remembering our friend was no longer with us.

The ride was a swift and silent one. Buford held onto my shoulder much like a terrified cat would. His hands clutched at the raggedy old tunic I wore. A gift from Thelgrim. Buford's heels dug in enough, I could feel the pressure from his tiny shoes. Aluwyn held on to my waist tightly. Her face pressed against my back. I could feel the tunic moisten and could tell tears still streamed from her face.

I couldn't imagine what she was going through. Being kidnapped and forced to watch as her foster father was being eaten alive by that monster. Though sadness choked at my throat, anger and rage burned bright through my chest. My hands tightened around Alden's antlers. I gave his side a gentle rapt with my feet. Goading him to pick up the pace.

When we arrived at Thelgrim's old shop. It was emptier than its appearance. It was like it had died too. All of Bramblehaven seemingly felt empty. Without the clanks of Thelgrim's hammer against steel, Or the roaring of his smithy fire. A once fascinating town seemed lacking.

I sat for a moment feeling its emptiness ring through my core. I watched Aluwyn as she dismounted and walked slowly about the smithy. Tracing her fingers on the surfaces solemnly. Like reaching out for a loved one, only to clutch at mist.

With the help of Buford and his predisposition to cleaning. We gathered up some of Thelgrim's belongings. Aluwyn chose which ones she was willing to part with. Among them, was a hand sketched photo of Thelgrim and her from their first goblin market trip together. She told the story of how the dark elf that drew it, kept grunting in frustration. This was because of course little Aluwyn was so excited she could hardly sit still enough, to have their likeness captured, and Thelgrim was such a patient parent. Instead of scolding her he laughed his big belly laugh and raised her into the air professing his love for the little rascal. She smiled for the first time in what seemed like forever.

A single tear drifted down her cheek. I could tell she was fond of this memory of them together. We gathered the pile of belongings and hitched a cart to Alden. We took them to the river where Aluwyn and I first got to know one another. The same one where I had learned of the clockwork flowers magic. As it healed the scorched land and brought the ladyvine back to life.

We unhitched the cart and pulled off the wooden flat of Thelgrim's belongings. Together we carried the flat until we gently placed it onto the river's surface. Aluwyn rested the hand sketched photograph onto the Pyre after kissing Thelgrim's likeness. We struck a match, pushing the Pyre downstream.

I wrapped my arm around her waist and held her close... We watched as the pyre became engulfed in flames. Saying goodbye to that lovable dwarf, the way he would have wished it. Releasing sparks of spirit and magic into the air around us... Remembering him fondly we held each other and watched his memory float away.

Aluwyn whispered, "Thank you" as she looked up at me. Silently she kissed my cheek. Walking over to the others, she sent Buford and Alden ahead. We chose to take the slow walk back to the old shop and remember our friend, for just a bit longer. As night fell, the lightning bugs flitted about dancing to the cricket's song. We came to the front of what was once Thelgrim's shop but will always be Aluwyn's home.

Chapter 12

KNOW THY ENEMY

Morning light trickled in from the window. It seemed brighter than usual. Like a renewal. I gazed upon the beams of light and watched the dust particles float like sparkles against the dark hues of the wall behind it. Aluwyn's hair tickled my nose as she was still fast asleep on my chest. I rubbed my face trying not to wake her. After all we were up late.

We had spent most of the night reminiscent on Thelgrim's memory. We drank pints of Centurion Cider. Aluwyn did most of the talking that night. I gave her an ear and a shoulder to cry on. She shared photographs, trinkets, and memories with me so powerful it almost felt as if Thelgrim was still with us.

At the end of the night, she didn't want to be alone. As soon as her head hit my chest that night, she fell fast asleep. My attempt at not waking her was to no avail. She looked up at me and smiled. *"Thank you, Ari. I haven't slept that good in a while."* She said sitting up. *"Sometimes you just need to let it all out. Things pile up, feelings pile up. It's good to unpack things now and then. I'm glad I could be there for you."* She smiled when I said this. *"The Cider helped to, how's your head?"* She giggled and held her palm to her forehead. *"Feels like a minotaur kicked me."* I laughed. *"Same, I'll make us all breakfast. Go get the boys."* She smirked patting my chest before getting out of bed. *"Got it."* I groaned sitting up.

I found Alden curled up by the forge. I gave him a pat on the head. *"Rise and shine my friend."* *"Must I? It feels as if I broke my antlers."* His echoed groans made me laugh. *"That's what we call a hangover, it's also why we don't drink an entire barrel of cider."* *"How was I to know, it tasted sweeter than a myrtle bees honey."* He picked up his head trying to shake off the hangover.

It took me awhile to find Buford who apparently made his home in the bread box. We gathered at the large oaken table. Buford sat atop a pepper grinder using its lever as a tabletop, similar to a highchair. Alden laid on the floor, his head held high. He was eye to eye with me in my sitting position.

Aluwyn gave us all some breakfast, serving Buford's on a big blue button. *"So, Buford tell me, do you remember things when you're a bogart?"* I inquired. *"That's a silly question, but yes of course. It's similar to a mood swing or what's the surfacer word... hangry? Yes, that's it."* He smiled from ear to ear and gave an awkward wink like someone learning the newest lingo. *"Oh, I get it, basically it's a temper tantrum."* I smiled and took a bite. *"Yeah, that's right. Spot on really."* He said kicking his tiny dangling feet back and forth. *"Alright, then may I ask you something?" "Yes of course, though I suppose you just did."* He grinned. *"What is it?" "Well, I'm just curious how did you end up working for that monster Aliester?"* The room fell silent. Aluwyn looked down. Alden stopped mid chew and stared pensively.

"Mm I see, this may come as a bit of a shock but that gruesome place used to be my home. You see I was king Darian's butler before his passing. I'm sure we all can assume what happened to him. But it all began when the vortex opened up in the sky above Telmara."

He paused drinking water from the thimble, next to his button plate. *"That weird man with the funny mustache came through and fell right into the courtyard. The guards immediately grabbed him and brought him to king Darian. He had a silver tongue and tricked Darian into letting him free. I didn't trust him from the start, but the king kept his company."*

"Why on earth for?" I interrupted. *"Darian was curious about the surface world, and even more curious about the bangle the stranger had, so was I. I was spying on him one night, when the stranger found out what it could do. He was tinkering with it like he did every night but this time it shot one of those collars out and it attached to the kings skogkatt. That's how it started. Once the stranger learned what it could do. He used it on Darian and took over his mind. Then he released Aliester."*

Alden grew increasingly agitated at his brother's name. He ruffled his feathers snapping up more boar bacon. He abruptly stood and retired back to the forge. *"You see he thought Aliester would aid him willingly, but that beast was even more devilish, and silver tongued than the stranger. He turned on the stranger, stole the bangle and captured his mind. He used the stranger like a puppet. While he hid in the shadows. Aliester took over the entire kingdom in just days. No one was any wiser, they all thought it was the stranger."* He began to look saddened. His legs stopped kicking and he stared at his empty button plate. Silence befell him.

"Buford? Are you ok?" *"Oh Yes, it's just he hadn't noticed me for some time. Everyone I knew was gone. Their minds wiped or they were replaced with greedy goblins or those bloodthirsty redcaps. I was stealing scraps like a mouse. Trying to stay hidden. I was so moody and hungry I was being too loud when I couldn't find a nibble. I was morphing in and out. That's*

when he caught me. Said he would eat me in one bite if I didn't work for him, like I did for the king.

This washed me with grief and anger. My feelings changed me into a bogart full time. Slowly going mad. That's when your strange friend brought me back. I really ought to thank him. And if I ever see..." his voice began to change, and his form began to morph.

"That no good rotten flea bag ill rip his tail feathers out, that slimy death breath ARGGHHHH" He flipped over his plate. A bogart once more and sped off wrecking anything in his path. *"Hurry we have to catch him!"* I looked at Aluwyn. She nodded and the chase began.

It wasn't long before I realized Buford the bogart and Buford the brownie were very, very different. From sweet and innocent to sour and devious in a flash. Buford flew up the stairs like a scampering rat, we were hot on his heels determined to catch the little bugger.

As soon as we reached the top step however, he slid past us on the railing laughing hysterically. Much like a child would as they glide across a waterslide. We fumbled trying to turn around. Aluwyn gave me a cute smile as if to say she was having fun. I smiled back, shaking my head as we continued the chase downstairs.

We lost track of him. The smithy fell eerily silent. We gazed around in the pause of the chaos. Looking for a sign, anything to point us in Buford's direction. Just then a bump and a clatter, came from the kitchen. We bolted towards it however once inside we saw no sign of Buford.

The kitchen was empty, but there was evidence he had been here. The cornucopia of fruit was strewn everywhere, cupboard doors hung crooked and open. Some of their hinges were ripped off and missing. A glass of water was knocked on its side. Drops of its contents fell to the floor into a pool.

A clue! Little footprints led from the tiny lake across the wooden floor. They trailed for a few feet before vanishing. Another bump and clatter followed by Buford grunting with pain. I can only assume he hit his head. *"Damn!"* Was the only word we heard coming from the utensil drawer of the countertop. I raced over pulling out the drawer quickly. *"I've got you now!"* I called out triumphantly. ***"Rrrrrr!"*** He growled then gave a devilish grin. This grin was a warning I should have heeded.

He prodded at my finger with a fork. *"Ouch you little!"* I shook my hand from the sharp pain. At Least he didn't break skin. *"Oh, like that do you? Have some more!"* He yelled as he jumped into the air landing on the silverware tray's edge. Catapulting an array of handcrafted elven utensils straight toward us. Forks, spoons, and butter knives went flying. Pelting us on our upper bodies and faces sending us backward a few steps.

These few steps were all he needed to make a break for it again. Just like that he vanished, and the scuttling sound of his feet died out. *"At this rate, we're never going to catch him Ari."* Aluwyn said, resting her hands on her hips. *"I suppose you have a better idea?"* I spoke with sarcastic undertones obviously a little frustrated with Buford and our failed attempts at catching him. Without a word, just a smile she gestured to a pot on the countertop. I looked over and was hit with a flashback.

Before I arrived in Underhill. Even before I had figured out how to open the Clockwork Flower. I was nose deep in a book titled, *"Faeries, Fae, and Magical Beings."* I recalled a section on what different magical beings enjoyed. It seems that most enjoyed the same exact substance that landed me in this strange land. ***Honey***. *"That's it!"* I said, kissing her forehead. We are going to catch him with bait I thought.

Quickly I poured the large pot of honey into a basin made from an old mead barrel. I placed the heavy trap of sticky amber liquid in the middle of the floor. I stood back and crossed my arms with a grin on my face feeling triumphant once again. Minutes passed and nothing happened. My cheeks reddened with embarrassment. "Uh, now what?"

Aluwyn giggled as if I had finally asked for directions, after being lost for too long on an unmarked road. She walked over to the wall and grabbed a metal triangle and rod and promptly rang it. I half expected her to yell out "supper"! Mocking the movies, I had seen about the southland. There was no need for that though, because when I turned around toward the honey trap there was Buford. I couldn't believe my eyes,

I was baffled. Here was this grumpy little bogart doing a backstroke in the basin of honey. Pausing only to spit some in a stream straight into the air. As if he himself were a fountain centerpiece. After witnessing this odd behavior, he gracefully dived into the bogart sized, amber filled swimming pool. Even stranger than that when he emerged, he was no longer Buford the bogart and once again Buford the brownie.

"Feel better?" Aluwyn laughed. *"Oh yes I do. Very much indeed. Thank you, I guess I was just a little hangry."* He said, giving me the same awkward wink as before. At that moment it almost felt as if I were home. The peaceful feeling subsided as Alden's voice bounced between my ears.
"Guardian, we've got company!" My heart thumped in my chest as we raced out.
We all gathered at the entrance in waiting, unsure of what Alden sensed just around the corner.

Chapter 13

RALLY THE THRONG

The sound of wearied footsteps tramped through the silence. Our eyes strained against the dark street trying to make out our guests. As they made their way past the bioluminescent foliage and fireflies. Their faces became apparent and alight. Staggering toward us, were no strangers but our friends.

Grinning and laughing in a triumphant manner. Grip and Iniko obviously had bonded since I had last seen them. Arm over each other's shoulders they swayed back and forth, laughing and singing like two friends who drank way too much at the tavern. Tilly and Titus followed close behind, talking quietly to one another. Hilda and Finn took their time in the back of the group. Giggling and murmuring sweet nothings to one another, as one can only assume.

. Joy swept over all six of them as they glanced toward the entrance of the smithy and saw us gathered in waiting. *"Ah it's good to be back!"* Titus announced with his arms raised above his head. *"Come friends there's much to tell!"* The triumph in Titus's voice brought warmth to my heart and dare I say, courage for what was to come.

We gathered at the large oaken table united once more. Buford and Aluwyn brought refreshments and sustenance. Once he and Aluwyn took their places tableside. The time had come to listen to the tales of their travels. *"Who's up first?"* I asked the room. *"Aye, that would be Grip and Iniko."* Titus said waving his hand in their direction. His feet kicked up on the table as he lounged backward picking at his teeth.

"Telmara is free from tyranny. After you left us in charge of lowering their defenses. Iniko and I went to work, and I gotta say Iniko is an artist." Grip said with a grin. *"Yes, yes,*

but Grip mastermind. Grip good with timing boom-boom sticks."
Iniko clapped. *"Boom-boom sticks?"* I asked quizzically. *"He
means fireworks. It was perfect.*

*Our first stop was into the city's waterway. That's wear
Iniko got the clever idea of using that magic bowl of his and sent
a mist up the grates of the waterway. It caused the entire city to
go into a trance. Similar to the soup incident he pulled on us in
the swamp. But on an enormous scale.*

*When we made it topside goblins and redcaps were
dancing to invisible music. We could walk past everyone, and no
one would bat and eye. From there I got an idea to scare em all
out of the city. That's when we went back to the citadel tower. I
pulled some fireworks out of my bag, that I had left over from
last year's Janus celebration. I fired them out of the highest
window we could find. All I could hear was 'dragon, dragon!' In
the streets, it was a ghost town when we left!"* Grip laughed his
impish laugh till tears welled in his eyes, as Iniko clapped.

*"Alright, alright you've had your fill its me and Tilly's
turn now."* Titus spoke above the merriment leaning forward his
feet coming to the floor with a thud. *"Tilly, the lovebirds, and I
were sent to the lost library to gather items and Intel. And here's
what we found out."* He gestured to Tilly who was standing
now... *"Shortly after the clockworks creation, and delivery. The
Dwartin fled Telmara. Fearing what was to come. They foresaw
the events leading up to this."* *"But how? there just cybernetic
dwarfs not magic wielders."* I interrupted with a furrowed brow.
"That's what we wondered as well." Titus interjected. *"It seems
our friends weren't working alone, and you'll never believe who*

they had helping them." His rugged rogue half smile egged me to ask, *"who?"* Tilly gave the answer that shocked the room…

"Merlin himself." "No way, didn't he die after the fall of Camelot?" I said in disbelief. *"Nah the old man was stuck in the in-between. He couldn't interact with your world or ours. No idea how he got out. Doesn't surprise me though, it is Merlin after all."* Titus spoke scratching his five o'clock shadow. *"So wait, if Merlin still alive it means he is out there somewhere, right?"* I wondered. *"It is a possibility."* Tilly stepped forward clasping her hands together. *"We found that the Dwartin went into hiding in the spire mountains. There's a chance Merlin could be with them. We also found out there's a failsafe if one of the clockworks fell into the wrong hands, but it didn't say what."* *"Alright, so we go ask them."* I concluded.

"What of Telmara?" Grip pointed out not wanting his efforts to go to waste. *"I'll take care of that; at first light we meet in Bramblehaven town square."* Aluwyn spoke up, the same fiery look she gave me when we first met. When I made the mistake of mentioning her clothing style. That look was enough to warn everyone not to question her. *"It's settled then, we will meet in the town square tomorrow morning and head toward the spires by nightfall. Is that enough time Aluwyn?"* *"Plenty."* She said as she flitted out of the room. *"Alright, let's get some rest we are gonna need it."* I announced. *"Yes, yes nice bed, no more icky ground sleep. Can do boss man!"* Iniko cheered happily as he hopped and spun his way out of the room.

When the morning light finally caught up with us. Its amber light filled every corner of that old smithy. Bringing the feeling of renewal along with it. There was something different in the air that morning. A courage, a togetherness we had been lacking. The ambiance of the room was filled with more Comradery. It was as if we were the fireflies that night in the swamp banding together to light up the darkness. Every movement made from one another was synchronistic. Whether it was Making our way through the blacksmith shop. Passing out breakfast. Or even getting ready to go. Aluwyn helped me into a jacket as we headed out into the brisk morning air and that's, when I realized it was as if this ragtag group had now become something more. They were family.

We made our way through the markets to the town square. Aluwyn directed Titus and Alden to fetch empty barrels of mead and set them up for her. She sent Buford and Grip to spread the word the town was to be gathered in the square for her impromptu meeting. Whatever those two did it worked. The townsfolk gathered in mass. Elves, goblins, dwarves, and hags. Circled around pixies, nymphs, sprites, and centaurs. A melting pot of faces all looked onward as Aluwyn stepped onto the empty casks of mead.

She quietly cleared her throat. *"Faefolk of Bramblehaven I beseech you."* I looked onward to the crowd of unsettled faces and mumbles as her speech began. *"We have all heard the rumors. A surfacer took hold of Telmara. Who steals Faefolk and forces them to join his ranks. We've heard he'd stop at nothing till all of Underhill is under his rule."* Terrified looks washed over those who had believed the rumors. And the non-believers shook their heads. One goblin shuddered and covered his ears. *"Well, today I put an end to those rumors."*

The crowd grew silent and curious. *"I know surfacers can seem scary, but those are just bedtime stories we tell our children. The truth is surfacers are just like us in so many ways."* She gave me a side glance. *"But what if I were to tell you it's not a surfacer you should be afraid of?"* She asked the crowd. Who grew more curious as to where she was going with this.

"It's one of our own kind. He is nothing more than a deranged and depraved peryton. Hiding behind the image of a surfacer!" She gave a saddened look to Alden as if to say sorry. *"Though my friends and I will assure you that not all surfacers or perytons are evil!"* She reached her hands outward on each side, ushering Alden, and I to step forward.

We obeyed. *"Some can even become friends!"* She followed up after the gasps from the crowd died down. *"The ones who've taken Telmara fled from us. Why? Because they are afraid of us. They know we have the clockworks of legend."* Awestruck sounds washed over the Faefolk.

As if cued I pulled the clockwork flower from my pocket and set it on the ground, to display proof. The others followed my lead. First Tilly then Titus. Followed by Hilda and Finn. Iniko was last. We stood like warriors in front of the townspeople.

"I know things have seemed bleak for so long but it's about to change. Telmara is ours again! Those of you who have fled, can return and those of you who wish, are urged to defend it. There's no telling what they will do next. Your family and friends who weren't turned have been freed. Go to them." Cheers erupted from the crowd. *"So, I ask of you: Who will defend the city? While we seek answers to free those under his control?"*

Like the magic of willpower Itself the crowd roared fiercely, ready to defend it with their lives. The sheer magnitude of courage emanating from them was enough to raise hairs. *"You must leave at once! Time is of the essence!"* As she finished. The crowd began scrambling to prepare. *"Not bad beautiful!"* I said as she stepped down. She smiled back. *"Thank you…"* Alden's voice echoed quietly as he rested his head on her shoulder a grateful tear fell from his eye. *"It's the least I could do…"* She said petting his neck. *"Now come on. We have some dwartin and a wizard to find."* With that, she began leading the way to our long trek up the spires.

Chapter 14

THE SPIRES

"C'mon this way!" Aluwyn called as she shifted her shape into her smaller pixie form. She zipped off toward the base of the mountains. *"Well, someone's in a hurry, we haven't even had breakfast yet."* Grip shrugged shaking his head. I chuckled when I said, *"Oh? Do you want to be the one to tell her otherwise?"* Grip gulped, knowing Aluwyn's fierce temper. Letting out a sigh he trudged forward.

With all of us reunited again. I felt comfort in this journey. After all what more do you need than good company to make an arduous journey a lot less daunting. I breathed in a breath of fresh air. My heart filled with hope as a smile stretched across my face.

A year ago, I couldn't even imagine a place like this existed and now I couldn't imagine going back. My life before was so much less fulfilling. I felt more at home in Underhill than I ever did in Manhattan. I wasn't sure I could return to the mundane city life.

"You're doing it again guardian!" Alden's voice boomed inside my brain. *"Doing what?"* I retorted. *"Thinking, so loudly. Quiet your mind be present. You never know what lies ahead."* Alden offered his sage advice. *"How do you do it Alden?"* I asked knowing it had to be hard on him. I mean his brother was behind all of this. It couldn't be easy. Could it? *"I do it because each passing second is a second closer to reaching our goal in stopping Aliester. If we dawdle it's a second closer Aliester gets to reaching his. Time is of the essence and focus is imperative."* Alden spoke this without diverting his eyes from the road ahead.

He had a point, however. We reached the base of the spire in half a day's walk. I had a flashback to when the plains beneath were scorched with dragon fire. We ate some rations and filled are canteens at the river.

Preparing for the road ahead. The ground of the spire mountains was coarse and grainy like salt. Resembling stalagmites in more ways than one. Pathways had been etched and carved into them long ago. Spiraling around them higher and higher each one connected to the other with a series of worn and tattered bridges. Nothing more than planks and rope. Each spire grew to different heights.

It wasn't long before I realized how dangerous this trek was. It also came with the realization that this place was a labyrinth. There were more spires than can be perceived from Bramblehaven. It was made clear as we reached the height of our fifth spire. Behind them was nothing short of a forest of these megalithic stalagmite structures. What was worse was the tallest one was at its center. I had a feeling that's the one we needed to get to.

"Can't say they lack in security eh, chap?" Finn offered jokingly seeing the worry on my face. *"You can say that again."* I smiled. *"Are we there yet?"* Buford peeked from my shirt collar. *"No little man I'm afraid we have much, much farther to go."* I patted him safely back into my shirt.

The salted winds picked up the higher we got. It wasn't long before the air stung at my cheeks. The wind was abrasive and unkind. The salted air chapped my face. Talk about rubbing salt in a wound. The light was fading. An orange glow lit up the peaks and cast light onto the debris filled winds. Like a tangerine haze.

"We must find shelter!" Alden called from the front. *"It'll be nightfall soon; it will be too dangerous to continue!"* Upon hearing this relief filled me at once. I needed out of this air. My skin burned so bad silent tears ran down my face. The tears stung at my skin too. I thought to myself how Alden was the luckiest of us all. At least he had protection from the wind. His skin was buried safely under fur and feathers. While the rest of us had cracked and bleeding wind-torn faces. Time in some shelter would do some good. Maybe Iniko could patch us up with some magic from his clockwork bowl.

It was easier getting lost in thought then being present with pain. I should have stayed present like Alden warned, because at that very moment the plank of wood Grip stepped on broke. He fell through the hole of the bridge grasping at the tattered rope. *"HELP ME PLEASE!!"* Grip called out but his hold on the rope slipped. Grip began plummeting downward. *"Noooooo!"* I screamed reaching my hand downward into the void of the orange mist.

Tears streamed down my cheeks. Sadness and rage burned in my veins as I watched his blue body fade downward into the orange mist. Finn and Aluwyn rushed to my side. Our sadness was almost audible in the overwhelming silence. A soft sound perforated the silence. It sounded almost like a wing beat. Followed by a succession of them growing louder and closer. Then the impossible happened.

"Yeeeeeeeeeeeehhaaaaaw!" Grips voice along with his body flew past us in disbelief. As he shot higher into the sky.

Riding on the back of Alden who seemingly came out of nowhere. They spiraled and flipped through the orange clouds before landing on the bridge at our feet.

"Why so glum, Chum? Can't get rid of me that easy." Grip gave us all a wink as he hopped down from Alden. Tilly pushed past us kneeling she squeezed Grip so hard I thought his eyes would pop out. I wiped the remaining tears from my cheek and smirked as Tilly kissed his forehead. *"I am not letting you out of my sight mister!"* Tilly said the worry heavy in her tones as she hoisted grip onto her shoulders. Akin to a parent giving a toddler a piggyback ride.

After crossing that bridge, we continued higher up into the next spire and found a cave etched into its rock face. It wasn't unusual to see. In actuality, many of the spires had caves along their paths. Alden told me, that they were left over from when the architects brought the spire mountains to life. When Underhill was young and blossoming. I came to find out the term architects were what many of the fae called their ancestors. Who sought out and created Underhill when they left the surface world.

Titus made a fire as Hilda passed out rations. Tilly clung to Grip, her love for him announced by her actions. Grip hadn't stopped grinning from the moment she kissed him. Buford raced about the cave frantically sweeping, trying to curb his craving for cleanliness. Alden sat at the cave entrance staring at the moon. Aluwyn curled up at his side. I joined them taking a spot next to Alden on the cave ground.

I cast my gaze toward the skies with them. Together we shared a moment being lost in thought. Alden spoke first. *"He is still out there; he must be stopped". "He will be my friend; we are all in this together".* I tried to assure him. *"Alden, can I ask you something?"* Aluwyn began, *"You may ask."* Alden replied, his gaze hung onto the moon. She paused and brushed at his neck.

"How are you and Aliester so different if you were raised in the same manner?" Alden let out a heavy snort and with a pause he began. *"Aliester from the time we were foals had always been a troublemaker. He rarely listened to father. He would sneak out and hunt before father determined he was ready to do so alone. One-night Aliester snuck out of the grotto we took residence at. I awoke at the snapping of branches and knew my little brother was up to no good. I followed him that night.*

It wasn't long till I trailed him to the outskirts of the small village of Perdita. When I arrived, it was already too late. My young brother gave in to the peryton instincts my father spent so long teaching us to control. I found him standing over a small Elvin boy and he had already had his fill of the boy's heart. The toxins had already reached my brother's brain and he stood laughing maniacally. I ran to his side questioning him and what he had done. I told him we had to tell father so we could get him detoxed and cure what he had done."

"Aliester looked at me with crazed eyes and said, 'if you tell them I'll kill them.' I did not heed him and raced home. As soon as I began to speak his truth, he raced past me. And in a flash mother and father laid still on the ground before me. We fought that night antler to antler. Rage burned in my heart like a thousand suns. I overpowered him and threw him toward the forest. The tree he hit snapped and crashed onto the campfire.

The forest burned white hot that night, like the rage we both had. Before he flew away, He told me he'd find me to finish the job. That was the last time I saw him or my parents alive." Aluwyn's' eyes welled with tears as she hugged his neck.

No more was spoken that night and we comforted one another, until our eyes closed on the moon. We drifted off to sleep. With the morning light we continued our trek deep into the spires; it was midday by the time we arrived at the central spire. Its winding path took much longer to traverse.

The central spire was the biggest and so each loop around took a considerable length of time. Though the pathway was much wider and accommodating. My friends and I could walk side by side, instead of in a uniformed line. As we neared its top, I could see a city of marble and gold at its peak. *"That must be where the dwartin live."* I spoke aloud. *"It seems more than the dwartin reside here my good fellow. We've got company..."* Finn nodded, gesturing to the perimeter of the great city. Posted outside it's gate was an army of white griffins clad in golden armor. *"And just what brings you here travelers."* A voice rang through our head telepathically. The only black feathered griffin stepped forth.

Chapter 15

MASTER MERLIN

There we were at the gates of this marvelous city. Being stared down by an army of armor-clad griffins. The leader of which had asked why we had come, and my mind went absolutely blank. I stood there with my mouth open. Half marveling at the beauty before me. Half stupefied by the sheer size of the guard poised to protect this magnificent city.

Finn came to my rescue seeing my awestruck face. *"General I presume, we seek council with the leaders of this city." "You presume correctly, General Galina at your service. You may enter but he stays here."* She nodded to Alden. *"But. He is..."* I began, Alden quickly interrupted. *"It is alright guardian. Galina and I are old friends..."* he said, pawing his hoof in the salt-like sands. Galina moved toward him, resting her forehead against his. *"It has been far too long old friend."* Galina said with somberness. *"Ages, my princess."* I swear I could see heartbreak written on Alden's face.

The gates swung open, and we made our way up the steps into the great hall. *"My mom would love this place."* I caught myself whispering. The architecture alone was astounding. It was as if someone had taken all the best things from ancient Greece, and Rome and combined them with Persian. It was breathtakingly beautiful. Though its modernization was evident.

Each room was sealed with heavy glass doors, clockwork mechanisms could be seen through the paneling. They silently whirred as they automatically opened and shut. Elvin scholars could be seen going this way and that. Some worked like librarians stocking bookshelves. Others carried parchment to and fro. The one in question was at the end of the great hall. Behind a desk sat a very stern, very snobbish looking elven woman, and she was not happy to see us standing before her.

"Do you have an appointment?" She asked haughtily. I started to say, *"No but it's very important we see..."* *"Achem I'm sorry no appointment, no passage. Good day to you."* She said dismissively. *"You don't understand, the fate of..."* she interrupted me again. *"I understand you don't have an appointment, out you go!"* She waved a hand at us without taking her eyes away from the paper in front of her. *"How does one make an appointment?"* Aluwyn interjected. *"By speaking with me of course."* The elven secretary rolled her eyes. *"Ok, can we make an appointment please?"* Aluwyn tried not to show her frustration. *"Hmm yes, the next available slot is in five minutes."* She said pretending to look at a full list of patrons.

"Ok we will take it!" *"Wait here."* The snobbish elf said as she disappeared behind the door. Five minutes seemed to pass like a lifetime at this point. We paced up and down the hall as time clicked slowly down. When the large doors opened again. The strange lady spoke once more. *"You will be seen now."* As she gestured to the door impatiently.

We went through in a single file line. Grip, who held up the rear, stuck out his tongue at the secretary as he passed through. Her disapproving gasp was audible through the door as it closed behind us. We entered a large circular room immersed in a blinding light. The back half of which was lined with a semicircular desk. Behind the desk sat fifteen empty oaken chairs. It looked more like a courthouse than the throne I had expected. The room was vacant.

Stepping forward I was beginning to think it was all a ruse. As we took our place in the center of the room. The oaken chairs began to fill with many wise and aristocratic looking figures. Some were dressed in robes while others clearly from the dwartin race were dressed in clockwork armor similar to Finn's. Appearing from behind a curtained door at the back of the room.

At the helm of the desk sat a very elderly man with a very long beard. His bushy eyebrows seemed to unfurl, and his eyes gleamed with a kindness. His closest consorts whispered to him. He raised two fingers on his left hand to hush the room. As the silence fell, we held our breath.

Merlin's gavel tapped at the desk. The silence that befell the room was deafening. The presence of Merlin himself almost demanded respect and awe. All eyes fell on this elderly wizard that was more than myth and legend. *"What a rather odd group I see before me, a pixie, an imp, a peryton, a brownie, a troll, a handful of interesting humans, and who can forget Finn. Who is no stranger to our borders. I can only assume you've come for answers. Is that correct Finn?"* Merlin rested his gaze onto Finn. As did we all.

What did Merlin mean when he said Finn wasn't a stranger here? After all, he had never mentioned anything. *"Yes, your majesty, we seek your counsel. As guardians of the clockworks, we look to you for answers."* Finn spoke. His eyes never left Merlin's. It was almost as if Finn had been afraid to look in our direction. I began to wonder what he was hiding.

" Ha, clockworks, where is your proof? Those relics were lost to us. You're nothing but Spies. Throw them off the

nearest cliff and let's be done with this!" Scoffed a very brazen dwartin. His scarred face and cold stare showed little interest in the matter. He leaned back resting his boots onto the court-like desk. In doing so he became more visible, and I noticed, His left arm was made of the same cybernetic clockwork as Finn and, "the artifacts" as he so elegantly put it. All the way from his shoulder down to where his hand would have been but, had seemingly been replaced with a steel hammer.

"That's quite enough Demetrious, let them speak freely without the interjection of your arrogance." Merlin waved him off. *"Arrogance! Why I ought a.."* Demetrious outburst was met with Merlin's own steely eyed interruption. *"Do what exactly Demetrious? Pick your words more carefully next time or I'll turn you into a cuckoo clock."* His voice never wavered from a friendly tone. It didn't sound angry but something about the way he carried himself told you he meant what he said. Demetrious choked on his own words as he slunk into his chair like a reprimanded teenager. My face reddened with anger.

"You want proof, here is your proof!" I said brandishing the clockwork flower. As I did so, the room filled with gasps. *"And as you can plainly see my counterparts bare theirs in the open!"* I gestured to my friends. Who all glanced at their clockworks. Titus however made a vibrant display. *"Ha-ha and I have this!"* he burst out, lunging forward holding the clockwork key like a fencing sword. Stifled and quiet giggling came from a blue sprite, sitting at the right of the elder's desk.

Titus looked over with a furrowed brow at the sprite but as his gaze fell upon her immediately his face relaxed into a more dreamlike state. I found myself thinking if this were a cartoon he would have floated into the air with big red hearts for eyes. Tilly kicked his foot bringing him back from his frozen state.

With that he stepped back clearing his throat. *"Ahhh, I see, but it's curious you only have six of the seven clockworks my boy. Wear might I ask, is the bangle?"* Merlin inquired. *"That's why we've come your majesty, it's fallen into the wrong hands."* *"More like the wrong hooves."* Grip interrupted me with a sarcastic mumble. *"It fell into the possession of a deranged peryton, he used it once already to take over Telmara. With the aid of one of the worst surfacers in our history. He has him under some kind of spell."* *"Not a spell, my boy the bangles creation was made to fire a control collar. Demetrious design if I recall."* Merlin said with another disapproving look toward Demetrious.

"It was forged in hopes to get blackguards and miscreants. To become submissive enough to bring in peacefully. However, I had a feeling this may happen. When I received visions of Underhill in ruins, I moved us here for safety." Merlin finished resting his gaze back toward us. *"In the lost library we found information stating there was a failsafe."* Tilly spoke up, stepping forward to address Merlin's court. *"Very clever my dear, there is a failsafe. However, it was never fully tested during its final stages. There's no guarantee it'll work, and it comes with a high price."* Merlin gave a worried glance. *"No price is too high to save Underhill!"* Aluwyn burst out in frustration, flitting forward in an upset display.

Merlin quite simply and quietly raised two fingers to hush the room before his eyes met Aluwyn's. *"This may be so, but the price would not be yours to pay."* Aluwyn backed down in embarrassment. Merlin stood motioning to the room to pay attention as he began his announcement. *"The matter of the failsafe has been brought to us. I can and will, teach these young guardians how to perform the ritual if and only if the agreeing parties accept the price. I ask the council of elders to place a vote for the sake of Underhill. Will we grant this request? All in favor stand with me."* One by one the elders rose. All except for two.

Demetrious failed to rise out of pride. He stayed slunk over grumbling to himself. And the other was an elderly imp who had so much white hair sticking out from his ears. I don't think he heard or had any clue as to what was even going on around him. He just sat eyes closed and grinning. The same thing he had done for the court's entirety. *"It's been decided, we shall grant you the lesson you seek but only if those selected accept the price of the ritual."* Merlin announced. Beckoning the others to take their seats.

He looked intently upon us. *"For the matter of the price..."* he paused *"...Aries Lacroix, Tilly Tremaine, and Titus Tremaine please step forward."* Merlin signaled to the three of us. We looked at one another, knots in our throats. We nodded amongst ourselves and stepped forward.

Chapter 16

DECISIONS

"You are not from this world, correct?" Merlin asked after a short pause. We shook our heads from side to side signaling that indeed we were not. *"And yet you wish to save it?"* He questioned, raising his bushy eyebrows in silent wonder. We nodded with agreement almost immediately. *"The cost of saving our world is a high price for you, though your choices are noble indeed. Once the ritual is enacted, your choice will be sealed as well as your fate."* He paused, stepping down from his spot at the court desk.

He moved to stand in front of Tilly, Titus, and I. *"To save our world.... You must become a part of it. That means, to you, the surface world will cease to exist. Your loved ones and everything you know will vanish from your memory. The doors to the surface will be closed to you forever and there will be no way for you to return. That is not all, because the magic is so strong it will also affect you physically. You will in turn take on new forms, fae or otherwise. The forms you take will solely depend upon the life you've lived thus far and what is in your heart of hearts."* He placed a hand on Tilly's shoulder and rested the other on the shoulder of Titus.

Lastly, he brought his forehead to mine showing he empathized with the strength of our emotions. Knowing it would change everything for us, the known and unknown. *" Now, I ask you don't answer immediately. A choice this big requires introspection. You may stay here in the spire with the scholars. I will have rooms readied for you. Though the answer is a dire one, and the fate of Underhill rests in your hands. I can allow you three days. At the end of the three days, I'll call upon you for your answers. Is that understood?"* A silent nod came from the three of us as we shared glances.

"Good, good." He stated, standing tall, he patted the twins shoulders and then ruffled my hair. *"You'll have anything you could need or ask for, while inside these walls. I'll be sure to have guards and scholars alike, at your beck and call. You need only ask. Now go, enjoy what the city has to offer. However, remember to keep close to your heart. For three days, can pass in the blink of an eye."* With his wise words, Merlin dismissed us by gesturing toward the door.

When we stepped out the light was blinding, it almost overpowered the senses. At least, it may have been the light that was overwhelming or maybe it was this new weight we carried. Regardless we had to squint in order to see, hands above our brows blocking the rays. I don't know about the twins, but my ears had a faint ringing between them. I felt dissociated from my surroundings.

The rest of that day was a blur. I was lost in thought, emotion, a sense that everything was incredibly overwhelming and heavy. When I walked my feet drug on the ground. I could tell the twins felt it too. There walk seemed much slower and heavier than their normal light-footed and quick demeanor.

Merlin was right. It was a high price indeed. Save Underhill and lose ourselves or save ourselves and forsake Underhill. Either way I had a knot in my stomach that wouldn't unwind.

I couldn't help but feel overwhelmed by the choice not only ahead of me but, also resting on the shoulders of Tilly and

Titus. The next morning, we three were inseparable. We talked mostly about our lives on the surface.

For Tilly this was like a dream come true. To become a magical creature in a mythical world was a childhood fantasy. She admitted some of her choice was made because of her growing feelings for our mutual friend. *"There's just something about that impish smile, and the way he changes color when embarrassed, and his cute temper tantrums." "Alright, alright we get it. Will you hush now sister, we're all very happy for you. However, we aren't as ready to give up everything we know."* Titus said, gesturing between him and I.

"Yeah, what about my mom in Manhattan?" I asked. *"Don't you miss London Tilly?"* Titus questioned. *"Miss London!? For what the smell? Yeah right! We were homeless, orphans. At least here we have a family, a home! Doesn't that mean anything to you?"* Tilly rebuked in fortitude. *"Well, yeah but what if I turn into some sparkly thing, I'm quite proud of my physique you know?"* Titus said, trying to reason. *"Is that all you can think about vanity!? Millions of lives could be lost, and you're worried about your pectorals!"* Tilly raged.

"What, you're saying you won't miss being human?" Titus spoke defensively. *"I'm not saying that! It's just a price I'm willing to pay for the sake of others!"* Tilly said storming off. Titus called after Tilly. *"Tilly, hey, c'mon wait!"* He followed her.

I took a seat by an ornate water fountain. Staring into its rippling waters. Maybe she has a point, maybe this wasn't the time to be selfish. I would miss Manhattan; I'd miss my mom. Even if I had returned, how long would it be till Aliester brought his self-indulgent war to the surface. They wouldn't stand a chance up there. I couldn't risk losing my mom or Manhattan that way.

I let out a heavy sigh. I found some resolve. We had to stop it here and now or everything could potentially be lost forever. With a mad peryton in power. I shuddered at the thought. Here's to hoping Merlin was wrong. I'd find another way back to the surface. I will see my mom again. There must be a way. Though even if I do, I would be different. I'd have to convince her I was still me, and there is the problem of forgetting her.

I knew what I had to do. I spent the next few nights compiling a letter to myself. Filled to the brim with my memories. I took photographs from my wallet. Lastly, I took the watch from my wrist, a present from my mom on my fourteenth birthday. I placed them all into a wooden box, I had asked a scholar to retrieve for me. The box would go to Aluwyn. If we survived this. She would help me remember. It had to work. I had to have hope when it felt as if everything would be lost. I let my hope guide me as I made my final decision.

Tilly had made progress with Titus over those final few days. Titus agreed to go through with it. All though now for whatever reason I'll catch Titus pretending to be a centaur. Almost like he was practicing. It made me chuckle to myself. It seemed as though we had our answer. Now it was time to tell Merlin.

We walked side by side firmly in our resolve. This time one thing was certain: we would set up a meeting with the snobbish elvin lady. No need to be shunned by her upturned nose this time.

Just as before the elders formed a ring around us in their seats of the court. Only this time it was just Titus, Tilly, and I. *"Your answers young ones?"* Merlin's feeble voice still rang above the court's idle banter, and silence fell as he spoke. Tilly who was very much the leader in this decision spoke up. *"We decided to proceed, your majesty." "Thank you, Tilly, but I must hear it from them as well."* Merlin pushed onward and his gaze fell upon me. *"I will do what needs to be done to save Underhill. I stand with Tilly."* I spoke stepping forward. *"And Titus what is your decision?"* Merlin's glance shifted to the rugged rogue.

"Aye, I'm in. I can't let my sister be roaming around down here without me." He spoke ruffling the back of his hair. *"Then it is decided, I will teach you the ritual. However, to work, it must be performed when in the face of great evil. So let us begin our preparations. You are to meet me in the courtyard, and I will guide you through the process."*

With that the court was dismissed. Heading to the courtyard we felt a new feeling of empowerment. Doing something for the sake of others instead of ourselves. Truthfully, I felt that was what being a hero was truly about. Though many things may be lost forever. I had a feeling that things were going to turn out for the best. We stepped into the courtyard were Merlin had seemingly appeared out of thin air.

"Let's begin, shall we?" Merlin announced gesturing to a circle of soil, at the center of the courtyard. Titus smirked his usual rugged half grin. Tilly was as giddy as ever, practically

jumping with joy. I on the other hand finally felt like the hero I was supposed to be. Smiling not only with my mouth, but with my eyes as well. The only thing left now, is to learn how.

Chapter 17

THE GATHERING

"The time has come, guardians. You must begin preparations for the coming battle. You've learned all that I can teach you for now." Merlin ended our session in the courtyard. *"He has a point, it's a long trek back and the longer we stay, the stronger Aliester may be getting."* Titus confirmed. *"You're right, Titus, but we still have no idea where Aliester fled to, after we stopped him in Telmara."* I voiced my concern. *"Time will reveal all that is needed to know, and as for your journey back. I am more than a wise old fool, gather your compatriots and meet with me in the west library."* Merlin spoke with a nod, ushering us out. We agreed to split up to gather the others quickly.

Tilly went to get Aluwyn, Hilda and Finn who spent most of their time in the gardens. Titus went to the steam baths to find Iniko, Grip and Buford. I went to find Alden who remained outside the city gates.

Upon my exit of the city. I saw no immediate sign of Alden or General Galina. I cast my gaze upward to search the skies. I didn't have to search long. They were making quite the display above the city. Diving, flipping, and swooping in unison. Spiraling through the air almost as one. You could tell it was a lot more than just friendship in full bloom. Like lost lovers reunited, now lost in an intrinsic dance. Unaware of the world below as they floated on cloud nine.

"Alden, ALDEN!" I called out waving my arms frantically. When he finally snapped out of his blissful daze and noticed me. General Galina guided him gracefully to a halt on the salted soil in front of me. *"It's time."* I said, patting his neck. *"General Galina and I did some scouting on our end. We spotted smoke by lake Cath Deiridh. The smoke has been growing daily.*

We are certain that's where Aliester is regrouping." Alden transmitted.

"We don't have much time then. We need to meet with Merlin in the West library." I spoke hastily *" Galina will accompany us and lend us her forces."* Alden's voice echoed in my mind. Galina bowed to reassure me of this decision. *"Thank you, we won't go down without a fight. We plan to rally as many as we can. Meet us at Telmara. I'm sure we will find some ground support there."* I delegated. *"You heard him! To Telmara!"* Her voice rang through the ether. The fleet of griffins stood at attention, before taking to the skies in a highly organized fashion. She quickly placed her forehead to Alden's before joining her team in the sky.

Alden and I were the last two to enter the West library. *"Ah, all together again, and it seems you've learned much since we last spoke."* Merlin said with a smile and that familiar twinkle in his eye. I smirked, giving a silent nod. *"And now, have we given thought to where we are traveling to?"* Merlin asked the room. *"Telmara, your majesty."* I affirmed. *"Very well, may I also suggest you visit an array of village folk as well. You may find far more are willing to join your cause than you'd think. Look to Finn for answers. He knows of the warriors in which I speak. For now, Telmara lies ahead."* As Merlin said this, he pounded his staff onto the floor. a portal opened behind him with Telmara in clear view.

"But heed my warning, do not rush into this battle blindly. Aliester is meticulous which means he has a plan and so must you. With that I wish you luck guardians." As we stepped through the doorway and into the streets of Telmara the portal

vanished behind us. Telmara was no longer a dystopian site; the city was alive and renewed; its streets were a melting pot of myth and fantasy. It put Bramblehaven to shame; there were races I'd never seen or heard of before. It reminded me so much of the Manhattan I left behind. Only, instead of people it was full of so much more.

Gnomes were riding on the backs of ladyvines like taxi drivers. Gremlins peddling watches and jewelry. Dwarves selling armor and baked goods. Sprites and sylphs shopping. Tiefling, kobold, and drow stalked the alleys. Hobbits selling cheeses and pottery. Fae peddling potions and enchantments. Giants and ogres were working construction.

I couldn't believe how far it had come. We made our way to the palace that replaced the once wicked citadel. On the way, we passed various street performers. Many of them were wood elves, imps, and fauns. I couldn't help but smile at their merriment. The palace was now guarded by Ursids. Though grumpy they were also honorable and noble protectors. The palace courtyard would be the perfect place to call for a gathering. Though it seems someone has taken residence in the new palace. Their permission may be required.

"Shall we then?" I asked the group. Tilly and Hilda looked hesitant and unsure. Fortunately, the rest nodded in agreement, and we pressed on. The Ursids granted us entrance and once again, the palace doors closed behind us. This time rather than a rage filled bogart greeting us. A pair of satyrs with pale gray eyes and an uncanny resemblance stood before us. They announced in unison, *"Hello there. The king has been awaiting your call."*

I found it strange how everything they did was in unison from speech to movement. Their pale gray eyes never even seemed to blink. *"Thank you, it's urgent we speak with the master of the castle."* I spoke slowly, wary of their odd behavior. *"Yes of course. Right away, follow us."* They spoke taking the lead through the main hall. *"Keep your eyes peeled. I don't like the feeling of this mate."* Titus whispered in hushed tones. I nodded in agreement as we pressed onward.

The castle was livelier than our last visit and its halls were filled with light. It cleaned up well, what was once gray, dark, and decrepit was now bright with gold, greens, and ivory. Plants grew happy and healthy at every doorway and not a speck of dust could be found. I couldn't believe my eyes how much this city and this palace had changed. Apparently, magic really does wonders taking years off a place.

Fairies flitted about the palace dusting. Female gnomes dressed in maid attire tended to the houseplants and the gardens. Passing the kitchen. I peered into the window. I watched with awe as a six-armed Naga was rapidly dicing away at a mountain of root vegetables. Just beyond the kitchen lay the great hall.

I expected we were about to meet the master of the reborn palace. However, when we came to the entrance of the great hall, we were halted by our guides. *"It is customary for you to wait here. We will announce your arrival. After the announcement you may proceed into the great hall."* The pair of vaporous satyrs stated, before leaving us at the door.

Their proclamation came in loud and clear. *"Announcing the Guardians of Underhill and its twelve kingdoms. Sent before your majesty with honor on high from Merlin Caledonensis, Merlin Sylvestrus, Myrddin Wyllt!"*

To our surprise the adjacent room filled with raucous applause. *"I didn't know we were being expected."* I said looking at the others who seemed equally confused. *"Well let's get this over with."* Grip stated, annoyed as always.

Stepping into the great hall, we saw before us an assembly of many cultures and creeds of Underhill. A mixture of every creature one could imagine filled the room. From fae to dwarven. Between bestials and elves no seat was empty. But every eye turned to us. Cheering our entry. In that moment we filled the farthest reaches of Underhill with hope.

A quiet, slow, and lazy clap came from the far end of the room. It made the applause all but evaporate, until all that could be heard is the metronome like sound. It came from a very pale, but spritely looking, elf lazing about on a throne as if it were a hammock. He stared dolefully at the ceiling of the room and did not budge. His long white-blonde hair fell to the floor behind his upturned head.

"Hmmph, the guardians finally returned to bless us with their presence." The elf spoke with a blasé tone. *"Well, it's about damn time! I was getting so bored waiting for some action!"* Like someone had flipped a switch his monotonous tone became enthusiastic. In a flash he was sitting like a cat on the throne, a grin from ear to ear. His canines were sharp and glinting almost as bright as the mischievousness in his eyes.

Everyone except for Tilly, Titus and I seemed to know who this strange elf was. The evidence was as plain as, the expression of awestruck on their faces. *"Awe, how cute! You don't know who I am! Wow it's been sometime since I was looked at like a stranger Hehe."* The strange elf chuckled whimsically. *"Does the name Robin Goodfellow ring a bell? ...Hmmm?"*

Chapter 18

BETWEEN MISCHIEF AND MADNESS

The room filled with silence. Waiting for our response but none came. *"Really! Oh wow, I thought for sure I was more well-known on the surface. But, seeing as I haven't been up there since I tormented little Willy into writing a play... tsk, tsk, Oh well... But I have an inkling you'll know me by another name..."* He grinned a Cheshire grin and gave a wink. *"I suppose you can call me.... 'pause for effect... '"* he muttered *"PUCK!"* He burst at the seams with whimsical laughter as our jaws dropped. *"Ha! I knew it. Stunned in my presence. How adorable!"* He spoke in a coquettish tone walking over to us. Before tapping my nose with his index finger giving yet another distinct and predictable wink.

"Come, come let's walk and talk, Guardians, don't be shy. You are in much too deep for that now. Besides I don't bite unless you ask." He rang in with eccentric laughter. We followed Puck to the gardens. *"Me big fan, big-big, big fan of Mr. Puck!"* Iniko shrieking, grabbing pucks hand and shaking at it vigorously. *"He's right, incredible work Goodfellow!"* Grip added with a ridiculous bow.

"Don't make me blush and talking about good work! How you two single-handedly won this city its freedom back with the old dragon trick, now that was amazing! It brings a tear to my eye really!" Puck chuckled. Iniko and Grip began blushing like a couple of schoolgirls at a boy-band concert. *"-And if you think I'm great, you're just going to love Rey!"* Puck fawned. Clasping his hands in a crisscrossed pattern.

"Who's Rey?" Grip said scratching his *head.* *"Oooo! You're going to love this; He is one of my many beaux. In fact, he is why I brought you out here! Hmmm.... I'm sure I left him here somewhere... Oh Rey-Rey! Where are you?"* Puck called

out with enthusiasm. Some tall grass in the far corner of the garden began to rustle. We shifted our focus to it. As an onyx-colored fox with nine tails bounded from the bush across the garden.

He leapt upon his approach. In mid-air he transformed from a magnificent fox into a very charming looking man. Dressed in what looked like French revolutionary clothes with his nine tails flourishing behind him. His piercing green eyes met mine as he landed gracefully back onto the ground. With a sly smile he grabbed Puck's hand and kissed it. His black medium length hair falling forward as he did so. *"Yes, my love, what can I do for you?"* Rey's French accent poured out quietly. *"Rey-Rey, meet my friends. Guardians this is Reynard. Rey-Rey, these are the guardians!"* Reynard took a knee. *"The honor is all mine mes amis. Reynard the fox is at your service."*

"You gotta be kidding me!" Grip's normal eye rolling statement was much more enthusiastic. *"Wow, no way!"* Tilly was giddy with excitement. *"I used to read your stories in the orphanage! The one between you and Bruin was my absolute favorite. It was so funny I'd giggle for hours."* *"Ah, you've heard of me. Well mademoiselle I can assure you it was much more than a tall tale."* He took a fanciful bow. *"Yes, yes. Rey-Rey is very clever, but he is also a strong council! So, we decided we're in! We are going to help. If not for the fun, maybe the fame!"* Puck giggled with delight.

If I thought two tricksters were too much to handle at times, nothing could've prepared me for four of them. It took a while to get them all settled down when they started going. Playing immature pranks on each other. Rolling around laughing until their stomachs hurt. It reminded me of a middle school lunchroom.

Though I had to give it to them. When they were able to maintain an iota of sincerity, tricksters really had a way with strategy and planning. Who would have guessed it? At first their plan sounded outright crazy.

However, it would be unexpected enough to really catch Aliester off his guard. He wouldn't even realize the trap set before his very eyes. After a very long couple of hours, we finally had a battle plan that we all agreed on. We were to gather our forces starting here in Telmara. From there we would have those who would join us spread the word to the farthest reaches of Underhill. Urging them to merge with us at lake Cath Deiridh for the final battle. At that point we would leave Telmara, making our way to Cath Deiridh on foot to hide our presence as much as possible from Aliester and his harpies. Keeping as close to cover as possible. Once there, Puck and Reynard's plan will go into effect. While our armies attack. Creating a big enough diversion, Aliester won't be able to look away. Letting us do what needs to be done.

"Well now, I got to hand it to you. You're making this look like child's play. Color me impressed!" Titus said with his usual rugged half grin. *"Indubitably, I must say, I think we have a plan worth its weight in gold. All that's left is to gather others. Which, I believe, would be best found in Renfrew, Wildspitze, the forests of Tzora, and Longmore, Karnuhim desert and lastly the mountains of Sabalan."* Finn announcing with his vast his knowledge of the land. *"Well-well, aren't you well-traveled."* Puck winked at Finn. *"Oooo I just love it when you take charge*

like that!" Hilda fawned over Titus, sending a glaring message to Puck that read 'back-off' loud and clear. Puck pulled away rolling his eyes.

 "So, are we ready to do this thing or what!?" Grip eloquent as always, spoke up at the perfect time. For a moment I thought Hilda may jump over the table at Puck, who was now making kissy faces mocking her. *"Finally, let's do this! Do you know how long I've waited to use this?!"* Puck flashed a Cheshire grin. Motioning to a small red box with a glass panel. The panel read 'break in case of emergency'. Inside the box was a tattered old rope. *That's strange what good is an old rope in this, or any situation?* I found myself thinking. I was about to find out as Puck nonchalantly shattered the panel with a single tap from his index finger. Without a second guess, Puck reached in and gave the rope a tug.

 The room began to shake, as a loud **Gong** rang from somewhere high above. A few small loose rocks fell from the ceiling. Not dangerous by any means but certainly dramatic. *"Wait! Wait! You're going to want to see this!"* The elated Puck ran to the nearest window overlooking the city.

 Pulling back the deep red velvet curtains, you could just make out the commotion below. As everyone in Telmara halted their daily routines and began making their way to the castle courtyard. A mix of concern, disbelief, and even annoyance, washed over the faces of the citizens. *"Well, isn't that just the neatest thing!"* The mischievous elf said breathily. *"Come on now! We mustn't keep my subjects waiting!"* he chortled as he danced out of the room.

"Not sure if I should call him queen or king at this point." Grip laughed. *"Come on."* I smirked giving his shoulder a light shove. *"We've got somewhere to be."* I said, as the group of us began to head out the door.

Grip was left standing there alone. *"What? I thought it was funny."* He said quietly to himself. Kicking at a pebble on the stone floor in silence. *"Wait! Wait for me!"* he called after us. We gathered in front of the castle facing the horde of worried and disgruntled Telmarian citizens.

"Hi everybody!" Puck called out with enthusiasm. The citizens just stared on, expecting and impatient. *"So, I know your all very busy but..."* Puck began. *"Oh brother, he can't be serious, can he?"* Titus muttered, clapping a hand over his eyes with the mannerism of a mock headache. I looked onward, as a few citizens began shuffling away. Waving it off as another of Puck's tricks, I assumed.

"Were losing em. Someone needs to fix this and fast!" Grip spoke from the corner of his mouth with anxiousness. I tapped Aluwyn's shoulder quietly. Giving a silent nod toward puck at his magically erected podium. He had dramatic flair. I'll give him that, speeches however were not his strong suit. Aluwyn picked up on my hints. Aluwyn took her chance and approached the podium. Clearing her throat to get pucks attention. Which didn't exactly work. So, this time she did it again with much more gusto.

"Aha, yes, by all means. This is not my area of expertise." He said gesturing to the podium. However not before a closing statement. *"May I present to you the lady of the hour, The beautiful miss..."* confusion swept over him as he leaned

down and whispered. *"Hey pretty lady, what was your name again?"* she leaned in and whispered back. *"Aluwyn."* *"Ah, yes thank you for that."* He quietly replied before standing to address the crowd once more. *"Miss Aluwyn!"* he said clapping. He sent magical fireworks into the air from the corners of the podium. As Aluwyn stepped up to the podium.

Chapter 19

TO THE ENDS OF UNDERHILL

"Citizens of Telmara!" She called for the attention of the now, very disgruntled crowd. *"We may have defeated Aliester here, but the battle is far from over!"*

That was all it took, and the citizens snapped to attention. *"We received word that Aliester has regained his forces and is currently readying his army at his encampment near Lake Cath Deiridh."*

She paused taking note of the crowd's emotional state. *"I assure you there is nothing to fear! We have a plan, but we are going to need your help, and the help of as many of Underhill's residents that are willing to take up this task!"*

The crowd began to cheer in unison. Aluwyn paused for the duration of their merriment. *"Together we will purge the land of this scourge! Are you with us!"*

Her voice rose to match the energy of the crowd. Cheers and applause erupted from every corner of the mob. There applause could be heard outside the city walls. *"Those of you who can fly, spread the word. We attack eight days from now, wait near Rynfyre Ridge till first light. We want to send a message to Aliester that he can't ignore! Gather our people from every corner of Underhill! From the mountains of Sabalan to the forests of Tzora, and Longmore. The cities of Wildspitze and Renfrew to the deserts of Karnuhim! Spread hope to its farthest reaches. United we march on Lake Cath Deiridh! Go, time is of the essence! We stand and fight together!"*

With her final rallying words, the crowd dispersed, and many took to the skies, flying in all directions. Aluwyn stepped down from the podium overjoyed. When she turned and saw Puck was sobbing quietly to himself in a far corner. She approached him, placing a hand on his shoulder. *"You ok toots?"* she inquired empathetically. *"Huh, oh yeah, I'm fine...'sniff'... It's just that was so...so...beautiful!"* cueing up more waterworks from Puck. She giggled shaking her head at his display. Turning and sending me an, 'I can't believe I did it' sort of smile. I smiled back with pride.

It wasn't very long until we set out for Cath Deiridh. Bravery in our hearts, in hopes that this goes as planned. The road to Cath Deiridh was long and arduous. It was the farthest we had yet to travel. Far to the southeast lay the enemy.

Grip, Iniko, Reynard, and Puck, stuck together like fast friends. They had a way of helping us all pass the time. You never knew what to expect. At one point their mischievous behavior brought out Aluwyn's wrathful side. *"WILL YOU JUST BE SERIOUS FOR ONCE! THE DANGER OUT HERE IS REAL! IF YOUR RACKET CONTINUES, WE ARE BOUND TO BE SPOTTED. SO, FOR ONCE WILL YOU JUST SHUT UP!"* It's been a long time since I've seen that side of her. It was safe to say things were quiet for some time.

I found my mind wandered more, of home, of Manhattan. I pictured my mom's face. I knew she must have been beside herself with worry. Though I bet if she could see me now, she would be so proud. She wouldn't be nagging me for having my head in the clouds. She would be so impressed with how far I've come, how much I've grown and learned. I know I am.

I suppose though, it would have come to this eventually, maybe not the magical adventure in a subterranean earth part. The moving on part though is kind of inevitable. At some point you leave the nest and miss them with all your heart. Unless of course your caught up in the midst of a battle, caught in some megalithic storm, maybe weather related, maybe just life being too much to handle. Though, in those cases I could still call on her for help. Down here, I'll never get to hear her voice again. I think that's what hurt the most.

In seven days', time, we reached Rynfyre Ridge. It was the best lookout spot over Cath Deiridh. The caves of the ridge would provide significant cover, from Aliester's watchers. We arrived just in time, as the battle is to take place at dawn. I scanned the horizon looking for something, anything to assure me we were ready. No sign came, however. So, either they were really good at hiding like we were, or we were alone out here.

I shuddered to think of us trying to take on Aliester's massive army by ourselves. *"Where did they all come from?"* Tilly questioned. *"Looks as though he has been busy too."* Titus followed up. *"Merlin did warn us."* I stated the obvious. *"We will defeat him, or we will die trying mes amis."* Reynard said standing from his squatted position on the ground. He was drawing up the battle plan in the dirt. We needed to be sure we all knew the plan and were ready for the battle to come.

Night fell, the world around us was quiet and still. The air was crisp with a bite that would sting your nose. We all gathered in the deepest cavern. No fire, too much smoke and to close to the encampment. Instead, we huddled around a bed of coal. It's faint glow barely perceivable from within the cave. Hot enough to keep us somewhat warm. Not too hot, that the glow would catch Aliester's watchful eyes in the sky. You could hear their terrible screeching as they patrolled nearby.

Puck and Reynard were fast asleep together in the corner. Finn and Hilda turned in early as well. Alden guarded the mouth of the cave, always on the ready. Grip and Iniko lulled to sleep sitting against the cavern wall. From where I sat, they reminded me of a couple of old fishing buddies asleep in rocking chairs on the front porch. Buford rested on a large stone near the coals, and Aluwyn was fast asleep on my chest.

Tilly, Titus, and I sat in silence wide eyed. Sleep would not come easy tonight. After all it was our last night being human. If Merlin's fail-safe spell works and we pull it off, we will be transformed by its magic. I suppose we were all lost in our own trips down memory lane. We must have dozed off eventually because, I was jolted from a deep slumber. When Alden returned from the mouth of the cave. *"Rise and shine guardians! The sun will not be far behind you. Dawn is nearly upon us."*

We met outside the cave to begin preparations. Puck, Reynard, Grip, Buford, Alden, and Aluwyn stood side by side on the ready for what was to come. It honestly, was a great plan. Reynard certainly had some amazing tricks up his sleeve, and this had to be his best plan yet. In Telmara we discussed the spell and how it would transform Tilly, Titus, and me. Though the spell requires all six guardians.

This triggered Reynard's ultimate plan if we were to transform so would they. Iniko, got to work throwing ingredients into his clockwork bowl. He gave his bowl a quick shake and placed it on the ground before them. He stepped back and stood with the rest of the guardians. As we stood side by side. Parallel to the other six, eye to eye.

I spoke in Iniko's stead to ensure that everything was said just as it was meant to be. The bowl started to rattle and move across the ground. Orange smoke billowed forth, with such a force that the cap of the bowl flew through the air. Landing at Iniko's feet. The orange smoke screen covered our six friends. When it cleared. We found ourselves staring at exact replicas. Puck coined it as, the false guardians. They would approach the encampment boldly from the front. While the real guardians' sneak in from behind.

Chapter 20

THE BATTLE OF CATH DEIRIDH

We were poised and ready, peering over the ridge awaiting dawn's first light. This was it, in that moment everything was silent and still. So much so my heartbeat was audible, and in time with the heat of my breath on the cold air.

The harpies no longer patrolled the air. There was no need now that the encampment below was awake and alive. Filled to the brim with Aliester's army. Orcs picked on goblins. Trolls picked at their nose's. Minotaur stood guard, unfazed by the surrounding debauchery.

I studied there every movement. Looking for the best route to Aliester's tent. The self-proclaimed king was likely to be staying in the enormous tent at the rear of the encampment. That was our target. Getting there may prove to be tricky however, Aliester's army was massive.

Sirens filled the lake. Hellhounds and kobold stalked the field in front. Ogres sharpened weapons. Harpies sat on top of wooden perches just outside the military tents. Naga and djinn sat around fires playing dice and cards. Drow lurked in the shadows. Redcaps were dying their clothes in a trough of fresh blood.

I'll give Aliester this, he had a way of preparing for everything, but nothing could prepare him for this. A single ray of light peaked over the horizon. With it, came the call of conch shell trumpets and bull horns. *"They came!"* I said aloud as the horns sounded from the left, right and behind our position.

The bang of dwarven shields and battle cries signaled the stampede. The skies filled with gryphons. Armored dwarves and ursine raced down the ridge first. Followed by elves and druids. Next came the city folk in all shapes sizes and races.

Carrying all manner of weapons. I even saw an elderly goblin wielding a chicken, blindly waving it like a sword.

"Time to put on a show!" False me said whimsically, flashing a Cheshire grin and giving a wink. With that, the false guardians took up the rear of the horde. Walking through the blazing battle below in a manner, that made time seem like it had slowed to a stop.

Aliester stood at the entrance of his tent surveying the battle in front of him. His eyes glued to the false guardians as they hacked their way through. Swords and shields crashed, harpies and gryphons rained feathers. Roars and yelps filled the air. It was time we did our part.

We snuck low to the ground around the river and into the trees. We made our way alongside the carnage of the battlefield. We had to be careful, but we had to hurry as well. The faster we initialize the spell. The faster those under his control will be released from their brainwashing collars, and the more lives we can save.

Two hell hounds were sniffing the air, near the tree line where we hid. Grip thoughtfully removed his left sock. Stained and stinking. He tossed it into the field, and they began to fight over it. Not only was it a distraction but it had a way of masking our smell, judging by the face Tilly made.

We pushed onward through the thicket. Watching the battle, I stopped. The false guardians still making there forward approach. I was worried about their safety, but they held their own, If not more on the battlefield. Puck made me look like a real champion. Reynard playing the part of Finn was merciless. You could tell these to have had their share of battle. Grip made a convincing Iniko, scaring off goblins with his wacky behavior. Aluwyn as Tilly was quick with a rogue blade. As was Alden, as Titus. They both ran down the battlefield swiftly and deadly. It was unmistakable that Buford was having way too much fun being a little big for his britches as Hilda. As he stomped and pushed enemies aside like they were fleas. He laughed maniacally with her voice as his own.

At last, we reached the rear of Aliester's tent. Carefully we waited to enter till the cue. I heard my voice call out *"Aliester! This ends now!"* it was in fact my voice, but it didn't come from me. Puck and the others must have reached the entrance. That was our cue. Who better to keep him talking than Puck.

While Aliester was preoccupied with pre-battle banter. We placed our clockworks in a pile on the ground encircling them hand in hand. *"Ah yes, now I finally get to tear you all limb from limb!"* I heard Aliester's telepathic threat toward the false guardians. It was now or never. We began chanting in unison…

Sword and shield,
 to protect and wield.
Locket and key,
 to hold dear and set free.
Flower of rebirth,
To heal this earth.
May the shackles that bind,
 release our kind.

At first nothing…, we only heard Aliester's clairvoyant chatter. *"Where might my brother be hiding, too scared to show his face? Pathetic…"* the false Titus had taken too much his voice boomed. *"What you fail to realize little brother is I stand before you even now!"* with that confession the mirage of falsehood fell away. Now it was Alden who stood face to face, and horn to horn with his brother.

Realizing it was a trap all along, Aliester cried out *"Noooooo!"* As he reared up and turned toward the backside of his tent. His realization came far too late, as a brilliant golden light burst forth from the clockworks. Spreading like snakes through the encampment and washing over Titus, Tilly, and I.

Latches were set loose with **clicks**, *pops*, and **whirs** parading the air. Aliester did not know whether to watch his deranged dream fall apart at the seams or look behind the curtain at his authentic adversaries. Caught between a rock and a hard place.

The winding light moved quickly freeing the enslaved from his control. Many waking to the forged and fraudulent fight forced upon them. Recognizing friends and relations. Weapons and shields fell to the ground with a clatter. Cries of merriment and anguish filled the air. For though they were free, some had loved ones who had fallen. Some never even dreamed of battle and were left with the shock. Though those that survived were thankful. Their roller coaster of emotion all stopped at the final station, and that station was revenge.

Aliester was surrounded. Not a single real ally. His false friends now set free, had a bone to pick with him. The golden light vanished as the last prisoner was freed. The veil that covered Tilly, Titus and I fell. Revealing our new selves.

Tilly shrieked overjoyed she had become a beautiful white kitsune. Her foxlike features brought out her compassionate nature. She hugged her three tails like they were a new blanket on Christmas Eve. It turns out Titus had hoped right. All his pretending to be a centaur paid off, and the best part for him was he got to keep his pectorals. We all laughed at his vain display of happiness. When he discovered how good he looked, as a centaur.

I was happy with my new appearance as well, becoming a woodland sprite. My pointed ears and nose fit my face. Though, the spikey hair would take some getting used to. I suppose it's better than the shaggy hair I had before. Time for self-discovery would have to wait. There was still a deranged peryton that needed to be dealt with.

We rushed into the tent, to see an emotionally shaken Aliester now trembling with fear. Titus, a natural born protector made a call to arms. *"Get him!"* Much to our surprise, Alden stepped in front of the cowering Aliester. *"Stop! This is not the way! He is nothing more than a sad, weak, and pathetic fawn. Hiding behind the ruse of power. He has no power now. Let him go. Leave him to his failure."* Alden protested boldly.

Knowing Alden was right, and it would make us no better than Aliester to prey upon the weak. I spoke up supporting this decision. *"Alden is right, we have won the real battle. Our people and Underhill have been freed from his tyranny. Let him go, he can do us no harm. Now that the clockworks have been destroyed."*

Aliester stood to his feet. The shadow he cast, showed a cowering man, dressed in what looked like an old German military suit, shaking with fear. Aliester paused looking up at us with hatred burning in his eyes. *"You haven't seen the last of me yet guardians."* His voice bounced off of our synapses as he ran. Disappearing out of the back of the tent. Like a deer running in fear from the sound of a hunter's gunshot.

Chapter 21

UNDERHILL UNBOUND

It's been weeks now since the battle for Underhill reached its peak. Things in this subterranean world were finally returning to normal for its residents. Tilly went to live with Iniko and Grip at the palace in Telmara. Puck and Reynard offered to teach the phooka and imp all they knew about trickery, and of course Tilly found love with Grip and wasn't ever far behind him.

Titus went to a tavern shortly after the battle. He went on and on about, having to see how much ale he could handle as a centaur. The last I heard he wound up in a drinking match with an Adaro pirate captain and lost by a single drink. The captain was so impressed he let Titus join his pirate crew of Grindylows, Kappa, and Nix. It's said that being the only centaur on board and inherently the strongest, He was made first mate and bodyguard for the Adaro Captain.

Finn promised Hilda, they would take a break from adventuring for a while. They moved out to Renfrew, where I'm told they are doing well. They found a very nice cottage to settle down in. Finn built a greenhouse in honor of his love and, plans to grow all the teal truffles Hilda could eat.

Alden received an offer from Merlin to come and stay at the scholar's spire, to help train their guard alongside general Galina. He tried to protest and said he needed to stay and protect me. I convinced him he deserved to be happy and should go. Besides, if he ever wanted to drop in, he was always welcome. He knew where he could find me.

Buford, Aluwyn, and I went back to Bramblehaven. Turning Thelgrim's smithy into a home. It took only days of being back for Aluwyn to restore some of my memories of the surface world. Though, it tends to get a bit fuzzy. However, I remember Manhattan and my mom. I'm sure that's what had meant the most to me, or at least I think it did. Like I said, still a bit hazy.

Aluwyn has also taken it upon herself to give me flying lessons. My first attempt made her laugh so hard it hurt her stomach. All in all, it was a pretty great life here in Bramblehaven. Buford kept the house tidy as long as we supplied the honey. We didn't want him to get too hangry. Though, it does happen from time to time. He can be a little bogart now and then but what can we say, we love him.

Yeah, things were going well until tonight. We gathered at the oaken table for dinner like always. Aluwyn made her homemade cream of mushroom soup with fresh bread. The house smelt amazing.

We normally kept our windows open like they were tonight. As we ate and laughed with one another, a strong gust of wind came out of nowhere. Along with it came a piece of parchment, folded into the shape of a paper crane.

The paper crane flapped and beat its wings as if it were alive, and gracefully landed on to the dining room table. It turned its paper head to look at Aluwyn, then Buford, and finally at me. With a warbling honk, it flapped its wings once more and unfolded into a letter. A letter which read:

"Dearest Ari,

I wanted to congratulate you on your victory over Aliester at Cath Deiridh. Though I'm afraid I must inform you the clockworks where not destroyed. They only disappeared, scattering themselves across Underhill once again. One

<u>seemingly came into my possession, and I believe it belongs to you. I've sent it to you, along with a gift to show my utmost appreciation for all you have done here. It will arrive shortly after this message. I'm afraid Ari, that I need to ask more of you. You must find the clockworks before they fall into the wrong hands. It's imperative that you do so. A close consort and friend of mine on Atlantis will know more. You must go there. Find the observation tower, and ask for Nikola Tesla, tell him Merlin sent you.</u>
<u>With utmost sincerity,</u>
<u>Merlin "</u>

"Wait, what the clockworks are still out there! Nikola Tesla?! Atlantis?!" I couldn't help but question. *"Oh Ari, does that surprise you!"* Aluwyn giggled.

Flush with embarrassment, remembering her words when we first met. *'Everything the human mind has written about or imagined is real in some form or another.'* I grinned and ruffled the back of my spikey hair. *"No, I suppose not, I could believe just about anything at this point."* We began laughing together. Buford joined in. *"What do you say guys, up for another adventure?"* I smiled.

Their answers were interrupted by a rapt at the door. As I approached, I heard a familiar **tick, tick, tick.** Ah, the package Merlin said he had sent, that really was fast. I thought to myself, as I turned the handle and pulled open the door… nothing could have prepared me for what happened next...

"ARIES D'ANGELO LECROIX, YOU ARE A LONG WAY FROM MANHATTAN. AND I DON'T REMEMBER

SIGNING A PERMISSION SLIP!" A strict tone emanated from her. *"...mom...MOM"*! I yelled.

We both smiled and embraced one another. *"You have a lot of catching up to do."* I whispered, *"I somehow believe you this time."* She smiled patting my shoulder. *"But that is going to have to wait, there's no time to explain. We have a trip to plan."* I said with a shrug. *"But I just got here! Where are we going? Ari? ARI!?"* My mom questioned as she came inside. *"Atlantis..."* I said turning to her with the excitement of adventure burning in my eyes.

Catching up would have to wait. We had a world to save.

END

ABOUT THE AUTHOR

Michael (M.J.) Stevens is a man of many hats. Podcaster and author of the new young adult fantasy novel "A Clockwork Flower." Michael spent his young adult years homeless and travelling, giving his characters some real adventurous flare! When he isn't busy writing his book, podcast or working his day job cooking. Michael is a dedicated and loving husband and father. Michael hopes of turning "A Clockwork Flower" into a book series, while teaching his son to chase his dreams fearlessly.